SCIENTIFIC AMERICAN EXPLORES BIG IDEAS

Evolution of War

Published in 2024 by Scientific American Educational Publishing
in association with **The Rosen Publishing Group**
2544 Clinton Street, Buffalo NY 14224

Contains material from Scientific American®, a division of Springer Nature America, Inc., reprinted by permission, as well as original material from The Rosen Publishing Group®.

First Edition

Scientific American
Lisa Pallatroni: Project Editor

Rosen Publishing
Daniel R. Faust: Compiling Editor
Michael Moy: Senior Graphic Designer

Cataloging-in-Publication Data

Names: Scientific American, Inc.
Title: Evolution of war / edited by the Scientific American Editors.
Description: New York : Scientific American Educational Publishing, 2024. |
Series: Scientific American explores big ideas | Includes glossary and index.
Identifiers: ISBN 9781725349513 (pbk.) | ISBN 9781725349520
(library bound)| ISBN 9781725349537 (ebook)
Subjects: LCSH: Military art and science–History. | War and society. | War–History.
Classification: LCC U27.E965 2024 | DDC 355.0209–dc23

Manufactured in the United States of America
Websites listed were live at the time of publication.

Cover: leolintang/Shutterstock.com

CPSIA Compliance Information: Batch # SACS24.
For Further Information contact Rosen Publishing at 1-800-237-9932.

CONTENTS

INTRODUCTION

During war, any technological advancement could mean the difference between victory and defeat. Both sides want an edge, and this technological tug-of-war has contributed to the rapid evolution of warfare and battlefield technology. Swords gave way to muskets; muskets gave way to machine guns. Nations are continually on the search for the next step in this evolution.

The articles found in this title look at the actual and theoretical advancements in warfare in the 21st century. Section 1, "Cyberspace: The New Battlefield," looks at the ways governments are trying to weaponize cyberspace. Cyberspace and the Internet have quickly become invaluable tools. But, from hacking a country's infrastructure to government-sponsored misinformation campaigns on social media, the Internet has become a favorite tool for criminals and countries alike. Section 2, "War of the Machines," examines the practicality and ethics behind deploying robots on the battlefield. Drones are a common asset in many armies around the world, from unmanned aerial vehicles (UAVs) flying over enemy territory to bomb disposal robots sweeping the battlefield for explosives. But this section also explores theoretical concepts, like cyborgs and robot soldiers. How can you counteract a weapon that you can't see, or one that can attack you from the inside? Section 3, "It Came from the Lab," addresses these questions by focusing on the long history of biological and chemical warfare. Section 4, "Science Fiction or Military Fact?," looks ahead to the theoretical wars of tomorrow. Many of the weapons that are commonplace today, like tanks and submarines, had once been thought to be science fiction. The next evolution of warfare will likely also take inspiration from science fiction, from the space lasers of *Star Wars* to Iron Man's high-tech suits of armor.

Section 1: Cyberspace: The New Battlefield

New "Symbiote" May Protect Microchips from Cyber Attack

By Charles Q. Choi

As microchips have grown smaller and more powerful, they have infiltrated virtually every corner of society, from smartphones to medical devices to the controls that regulate rail lines, power grids and water treatment facilities. Computer security experts have been warning that these embedded computers are highly vulnerable to attack because they are increasingly networked with other computers and because they have virtually no defenses protecting their firmware, programs that are hardwired onto the chip. In October, following a wave of network attacks believed to have originated in Iran, Secretary of Defense Leon Panetta warned that a "cyber Pearl Harbor" could be imminent.

Security experts used to take firmware for granted, notes Scott Borg, director of the nonprofit Cyber Consequences Unit, because, unlike software, it was designed to operate unchanged for long periods of time. "Yet the circuits embodying these programs are designed to accept a significant number of rewrites, so they can still be altered by cyberattackers," he says.

Engineers are making headway in protecting these chips. One new approach, described at a computer security conference in July, is a program that would scan random chunks of firmware code to check for signs of intrusion. Developers Ang Cui and Sal Stolfo of Columbia University say their "symbiote" can work with any type of firmware without slowing a computer's processing speed. It may also detect malware that no one had any way of noticing before, potentially shedding light on an "untold chapter of the history of Internet warfare," Cui says. They plan to deliver a prototype for U.S. government testing by the end of 2012.

Borg calls Stolfo and Cui's approach "very promising." Marc Dacier, a senior director at Symantec Research Labs, asserts that a major obstacle to any defense measure is getting companies to adopt it. The Pentagon is pushing for legislation to require the private sector to cooperate with government on cybersecurity issues. Without such legislation, Panetta said in his October speech, "we are, and we will be, vulnerable."

About the Author

Charles Q. Choi is a frequent contributor to Scientific American. *His work has also appeared in* The New York Times, Science, Nature, Wired, *and* LiveScience, *among others. In his spare time, he has traveled to all seven continents.*

The Fog of Cyberwar: What Are the Rules of Engagement?

By Larry Greenemeier

There is speculation among some politicians and pundits that the fog of war will soon extend to the Internet, if it has not done so already, given a recent report that the U.S. Department of Defense will introduce its first cyberwarfare doctrine this month, combined with similar announcements from the governments of Australia, China and the U.K. (not to mention Google's ongoing cyber spat with China). Less clear, however, are the rules of engagement–such as what constitutes an act of cyberwar as opposed to the cyberattacks that take place on government computers every day and who, if anyone, should mediate such disputes.

Wars have traditionally been waged between nations or clearly defined groups that officially declare themselves in conflict. This has yet to happen openly on the Internet, although such accusations have been leveled against China, Russia and other nations, says Chris Bronk, an information technology policy research fellow at Rice University's James A. Baker III Institute for Public Policy in Houston and a former U.S. State Department diplomat.

Cyberwarfare is more likely to reflect the wars fought against shadowy terrorist networks such as al-Qaeda as opposed to conflicts between uniformed national military forces. "One thing about war is that, historically, the lines have been drawn and there is an understanding of who the enemy is," says David M. Nicol, director of the Information Trust Institute at the University of Illinois at Urbana-Champaign. "When a cyberattack occurs against a sovereign state, who do you declare war on?"

The Defense Department is expected to clarify at least some of these gray areas when it releases its cyberwarfare doctrine, the *Wall Street Journal* reported last month. This would not be the Pentagon's first foray into managing cyberwar. The U.S. Strategic

Command's U.S. Cyber Command (USCYBERCOM) division has been operational since October and is designed to centralize the administration of cyberspace operations, organize existing cyber resources and synchronize defense of U.S. military networks. What is missing is a clear set of publicly declared rules under which USCYBERCOM will operate, Bronk says, adding, "We can't say there is a cyber command and then not have rules of the road like you do for other areas of military conduct."

Other countries seem to be following suit. The U.K. is developing a cyberweapons program that will give ministers an attacking capability to help counter growing threats to national security from cyberspace, the *Guardian* reported last month. Australia is also on record as saying it will create the country's first national cybersecurity strategy to confront the growing threat posed by electronic espionage, theft and state-sponsored cyberattack, the *Sydney Morning Herald* recently reported. Not to be left out, China has also set up a specialized online "Blue Army" unit that it claims will protect the People's Liberation Army from outside attacks, according to News Track India.

The inability of governments, or any other cybersecurity experts for that matter, to pinpoint the origin of cyberattacks is problematic and boils down to an intelligence problem, Nicol says. "Right now, with the infrastructure that we have it's very difficult using purely technological means to trace the source of some kind of attack," he adds. "You can't just look at the connection between one computer and another because cyberattackers use multiple levels of cutout servers that make it difficult to determine where data is being sent. These computers that do the cutoffs are in foreign countries so there's little recourse in terms of requesting log files from those computers."

This lack of clarity is troubling. "We're nowhere near where our policy makers believe we are or want us to think we are," says Anup Ghosh, a research professor and chief scientist at George Mason University's Center for Secure Information Systems in Fairfax, Va. "Internet Protocol (IP) was never designed with strong attribution properties. There's no connection between an IP address and an individual."

In cyberspace, it is easy to masquerade as someone else. "As naked as we are in security, so is China," says Ghosh, also co-founder and CEO of cybersecurity technology maker Invincea. "Their security might even be worse than ours, which is pretty sad. It wouldn't be hard to use China as a jumping-off point if you're in organized crime or another nation state looking to cause some saber rattling between China and the U.S."

Much of the U.S.'s current tension with China comes from Google's claims that recent hacker attempts to steal Gmail user passwords appeared to have originated from China. "Google is a very secure company, so when they are attacked we should stand up and take notice," says O. Sami Saydjari, a former Pentagon cyber expert who now runs a consultancy called Cyber Defense Agency. At the national level, however, "clearly you want to be able to attribute an attack with a degree of certainty before you respond with military action," he adds.

Internet agencies such as the Internet Corporation for Assigned Names and Numbers (ICANN) might be a reasonable place to start when trying to improve cybersecurity and avoid international cyberconflicts, but essentially this is a problem requiring input from the U.S. State Department and international policy makers and perhaps even something along the lines of an Internet Geneva Convention, Saydjari says. "One option is to make countries [that are] unwilling to trace the source of cyberattacks coming from within their borders accountable for the results of those attacks," he adds. "We also need more think tanks in this space such [as] we had during the cold war, where analysts discussed the consequences of nuclear weapons and mutually assured destruction."

If the U.S. chooses to enter a new war with another country within the next decade, there will be cyberweapons deployed under the guidance of cyberdoctrine to scramble communications and otherwise disrupt the enemy, Bronk says. "I would assume that the cyberattacks that we would consider as acts of warfare would be clandestine in nature, with Stuxnet being an example of how this might happen," he adds, referring to the highly sophisticated Microsoft Windows computer worm that made headlines last year when it attacked targets in Iran, leading to speculation that it was developed by the U.S. or Israel.

The threat of cyberwar "is like any great security problem; the key is not to either overreact or underreact but [to] have a calibrated response based on the knowledge we hold," Bronk says. "The problem is our knowledge is very, very limited. This is the infancy of this issue."

About the Author

Larry Greenemeier is the associate editor of technology for Scientific American, *covering a variety of tech-related topics, including biotech, computers, military tech, nanotech and robots.*

Hacking the Lights Out: The Computer Virus Threat to the Electrical Grid

By David M. Nicol

Last year word broke of a computer virus that had managed to slip into Iran's highly secure nuclear enrichment facilities. Most viruses multiply without prejudice, but the Stuxnet virus had a specific target in its sights–one that is not connected to the Internet. Stuxnet was planted on a USB stick that was handed to an unsuspecting technician, who plugged it into a computer at a secure facility. Once inside, the virus spread silently for months, searching for a computer that was connected to a prosaic piece of machinery: a programmable logic controller, a special-purpose collection of microelectronics that commonly controls the cogs of industry–valves, gears, motors and switches. When Stuxnet identified its prey, it slipped in, unnoticed, and seized control.

The targeted controllers were attached to the centrifuges at the heart of Iran's nuclear ambitions. Thousands of these centrifuges are needed to process uranium ore into the highly enriched uranium needed to create a nuclear weapon. Under normal operating conditions, the centrifuges spin so fast that their outer edges travel just below the speed of sound. Stuxnet bumped this speed up to nearly 1,000 miles per hour, past the point where the rotor would likely fly apart, according to a December report by the Institute for Science and International Security. At the same time, Stuxnet sent false signals to control systems indicating that everything was normal. Although the total extent of the damage to Iran's nuclear program remains unclear, the report notes that Iran had to replace about 1,000 centrifuges at its Natanz enrichment facility in late 2009 or early 2010.

Stuxnet demonstrates the extent to which common industrial machines are vulnerable to the threat of electronic attack. The virus targeted and destroyed supposedly secure equipment while evading detection for months. It provides a dispiriting blueprint for how a rogue state or terrorist group might use similar technology against critical civilian infrastructure anywhere in the world.

Unfortunately, the electrical power grid is easier to break into than any nuclear enrichment facility. We may think of the grid as one gigantic circuit, but in truth the grid is made from thousands of components hundreds of miles apart acting in unerring coordination. The supply of power flowing into the grid must rise and fall in lockstep with demand. Generators must dole their energy out in precise coordination with the 60-cycle-per-second beat that the rest of the grid dances to. And while the failure of any single component will have limited repercussions to this vast circuit, a coordinated cyberattack on multiple points in the grid could damage equipment so extensively that our nation's ability to generate and deliver power would be severely compromised for weeks–perhaps even months.

Considering the size and complexity of the grid, a coordinated attack would probably require significant time and effort to mount. Stuxnet was perhaps the most advanced computer virus ever seen, leading to speculation that it was the work of either the Israeli or U.S. intelligence agencies–or both. But Stuxnet's code is now available on the Internet, raising the chance that a rogue group could customize it for an attack on a new target. A less technologically sophisticated group such as al Qaeda probably does not have the expertise to inflict significant damage to the grid at the moment, but black hat hackers for hire in China or the former Soviet Union might. It is beyond time we secured the country's power supply.

The Break-In

A year ago I took part in a test exercise that centered on a fictitious cyberattack on the grid. Participants included representatives from utility companies, U.S. government agencies and the military. (Military bases rely on power from the commercial grid, a fact that has not escaped the Pentagon's notice.) In the test scenario, malicious agents hacked into a number of transmission substations, knocking out the specialized and expensive devices that ensure voltage stays constant as electricity flows across long high-power transmission lines. By the end of the exercise half a dozen devices had been destroyed, depriving power to an entire Western state for several weeks.

Computers control the grid's mechanical devices at every level, from massive generators fed by fossil fuels or uranium all the way down to the transmission lines on your street. Most of these computers use common operating systems such as Windows and Linux, which makes them as vulnerable to malware as your desktop PC is. Attack code such as Stuxnet is successful for three main reasons: these operating systems implicitly trust running software to be legitimate; they often have flaws that admit penetration by a rogue program; and industrial settings often do not allow for the use of readily available defenses.

Even knowing all this, the average control system engineer would have once dismissed out of hand the possibility of remotely launched malware getting close to critical controllers, arguing that the system is not directly connected to the Internet. Then Stuxnet showed that control networks with no permanent connection to anything else are still vulnerable. Malware can piggyback on a USB stick that technicians plug into the control system, for example. When it comes to critical electronic circuits, even the smallest back door can let an enterprising burglar in.

Consider the case of a transmission substation, a waypoint on electricity's journey from power plant to your home. Substations take in high-voltage electricity coming from one or more power plants, reduce the voltage and split the power into multiple output lines for local distribution. A circuit breaker guards each of these lines, standing ready to cut power in case of a fault. When one output line's breaker trips, all of the power it would have carried flows to the remaining lines. It is not hard to see that if all the lines are carrying power close to their capacity, then a cyberattack that trips out half of the output lines and keeps the remaining ones in the circuit may overload them.

These circuit breakers have historically been controlled by devices connected to telephone modems so that technicians can dial in. It is not difficult to find those numbers; hackers invented programs 30 years ago to dial up all phone numbers within an exchange and make note of the ones to which modems respond. Modems in substations often have a unique message in their dial-up response that reveals their function. Coupled with weak means of authentication (such as well-known passwords or no passwords at all), an attacker can use these modems to break into a substation's network. From there it may be possible to change device configurations so that a danger condition that would otherwise open a circuit breaker to protect equipment gets ignored.

New systems are not necessarily more secure than modems. Increasingly, new devices deployed in substations may communicate with one another via low-powered radio, which does not stop at the boundaries of the substation. An attacker can reach the network simply by hiding in nearby bushes with his computer. Encrypted Wi-Fi networks are more secure, but a sophisticated attacker can still crack their encryption using readily available software tools. From here he can execute a man-in-the-middle attack that causes all communication between two legitimate devices to pass through his computer or fool other devices into accepting his computer as legitimate. He can craft malicious control messages that hijack the circuit breakers–tripping a carefully chosen few to overload the other lines perhaps or making sure they do not trip in an emergency.

Once an intruder or malware sneaks in through the back door, its first step is usually to spread as widely as possible. Stuxnet again illustrates some of the well-known strategies. It proliferated by using an operating system mechanism called autoexec. Windows computers read and execute the file named AUTOEXEC.BAT every time a new user logs in. Typically the program locates printer drivers, runs a virus scan or performs other basic functions. Yet Windows assumes that any program with the right name is trusted code. Hackers thus find ways to alter the AUTOEXEC.BAT file so that it runs the attackers' code.

Attackers can also use clever methods that exploit the economics of the power industry. Because of deregulation, competing utilities share responsibility for grid operation. Power is generated, transmitted and distributed under contracts obtained in online auctions. These markets operate at multiple timescales–one market might trade energy for immediate delivery and another for tomorrow's needs. A utility's business unit must have a constant flow of real-time information from its operations unit to make smart trades. (And vice versa: operations need to know how much power they need to produce to fulfill the business unit's orders.) Here the vulnerability lies. An enterprising hacker might break into the business network, ferret out user names and passwords, and use these stolen identities to access the operations network.

Other attacks might spread by exploiting the small programs called scripts that come embedded in files. These scripts are ubiquitous–PDF files routinely contain scripts that aid in file display, for example–but they are also a potential danger. One computer security company recently estimated that more than 60 percent of all targeted attacks use scripts buried in PDF files. Simply reading a corrupted file may admit an attacker onto your computer.

Consider the hypothetical case where a would-be grid attacker first penetrates the Web site of a software vendor and replaces an online manual with a malicious one that appears exactly like the first. The cyberattacker then sends an engineer at the power plant a forged e-mail that tricks the engineer into fetching and opening the booby-trapped manual. Just by going online to download an updated software manual, the unwitting engineer opens his power plant's gates to the Trojan horse. Once inside, the attack begins.

Search and Destroy

An intruder on a control network can issue commands with potentially devastating results. In 2007 the Department of Homeland Security staged a cyberattack code-named Aurora at the Idaho National Laboratory. During the exercise, a researcher posing as a malicious hacker burrowed his way into a network connected to a medium-size power generator. Like all generators, it creates alternating current operating at almost exactly 60 cycles per second. In every cycle, the flow of electrons starts out moving in one direction, reverses course, and then returns to its original state. The generator has to be moving electrons in exactly the same direction at exactly the same time as the rest of the grid.

During the Aurora attack, our hacker issued a rapid succession of on/off commands to the circuit breakers of a test generator at the laboratory. This pushed it out of sync with the power grid's own oscillations. The grid pulled one way, the generator another. In effect, the generator's mechanical inertia fought the grid's electrical inertia. The generator lost. Declassified video shows the hulking steel machine shuddering as though a train hit the building. Seconds later steam and smoke fill the room.

Industrial systems can also fail when they are pushed beyond their limits—when centrifuges spin too fast, they disintegrate. Similarly, an attacker could make an electric generator produce a surge of power that exceeds the limit of what the transmission lines can carry. Excess power would then have to escape as heat. Enough excess over a long enough period causes the line to sag and eventually to melt. If the sagging line comes into contact with anything—a tree, a billboard, a house—it could create a massive short circuit.

Protection relays typically prevent these shorts, but a cyberattack could interfere with the working of the relays, which means damage would be done. Furthermore, a cyberattack could also alter the information going to the control station, keeping operators from knowing that anything is amiss. We have all seen the movies where crooks send a false video feed to a guard.

Control stations are also vulnerable to attack. These are command and control rooms with huge displays, like the war room in *Dr. Strangelove*. Control station operators use the displays to monitor data gathered from the substations, then issue commands to change substation control settings. Often these stations are responsible for monitoring hundreds of substations spread over a good part of a state.

Data communications between the control station and substations use specialized protocols that themselves may have vulnerabilities. If an intruder succeeds in launching a man-in-the-middle attack, that individual can insert a message into an exchange (or corrupt an existing message) that causes one or both of the computers at either end to fail. An attacker can also try just injecting a properly formatted message that is out of context–a digital non sequitur that crashes the machine.

Attackers could also simply attempt to delay messages traveling between control stations and the substations. Ordinarily the lag time between a substation's measurement of electricity flow and the control station's use of the data to adjust flows is small–otherwise it would be like driving a car and seeing only where you were 10 seconds ago. (This kind of lack of situational awareness was a contributor to the Northeast Blackout of 2003.)

Many of these attacks do not require fancy software such as Stuxnet but merely the standard hacker's tool kit. For instance, hackers frequently take command over networks of thousands or even millions of ordinary PCs (a botnet), which they then instruct to do their bidding. The simplest type of botnet attack is to flood an ordinary Web site with bogus messages, blocking or slowing the ordinary flow of information. These "denial of service" attacks could also be used to slow traffic moving between the control station and substations.

Botnets could also take root in the substation computers themselves. At one point in 2009 the Conficker botnet had insinuated itself into 10 million computers; the individuals, as yet unknown, who control it could have ordered it to erase the hard drives of every computer in the network, on command. A botnet such as Conficker could establish itself within substations and then have its controller direct them simultaneously to do anything at any time. According to a 2004 study by researchers at Pennsylvania State University and the National Renewable Energy Laboratory in Golden, Colo., an attack that incapacitated a carefully chosen minority of all transmission substations–about 2 percent, or 200 in total–would bring down 60 percent of the grid. Losing 8 percent would trigger a nationwide blackout.

What to Do

When Microsoft learns of a potential security liability in its Windows software, it typically releases a software patch. Individual users and IT departments the world over download the patch, update their software and protect themselves from the threat. Unfortunately, things are not that simple on the grid.

Whereas the power grid uses the same type of off-the-shelf hardware and software as the rest of the world, IT managers at power stations cannot simply patch the faulty software when bugs crop up. Grid control systems cannot come down for three hours every week for maintenance; they have to run continuously. Grid operators also have a deep-rooted institutional conservatism. Control networks have been in place for a long time, and operators are familiar and comfortable with how they work. They tend to avoid anything that threatens availability or might interfere with ordinary operations.

In the face of a clear and present danger, the North American Electric Reliability Corporation (NERC), an umbrella body of grid operators, has devised a set of standards designed to protect critical infrastructure. Utilities are now required to identify their critical assets and demonstrate to NERC-appointed auditors that they can protect them from unauthorized access.

Yet security audits, like financial audits, cannot possibly be exhaustive. When an audit does go into technical details, it does so only selectively. Compliance is in the eye of the auditor.

The most common protection strategy is to employ an electronic security perimeter, a kind of cybersecurity Maginot line. The first line of defense is a firewall, a device through which all electronic messages pass. Each message has a header indicating where it came from, where it is going, and what protocol is used to interpret the message. Based on this information, the firewall allows some messages through and stops others. An auditor's job is partly to make sure the firewalls in a utility are configured properly so that they do not let any unwanted traffic in or out. Typically the auditors would identify a few critical assets, get a hold of the firewall configuration files, and attempt to sort through by hand the ways in which a hacker might be able to break through the firewall.

Firewalls, though, are so complex that it is difficult for an auditor to parse all the myriad possibilities. Automated software tools might help. Our team at the University of Illinois at Urbana-Champaign has developed the Network Access Policy Tool, which is just now being used by utilities and assessment teams. The software needs only a utility's firewall configuration files–it does not even have to connect to the network. Already it has found a number of unknown or long-forgotten pathways that attackers might have exploited.

The doe has come out with a roadmap that lays out a strategy for enhancing grid security by 2015. (A revision due this year extends this deadline to 2020.) One focus: creating a system that recognizes an intrusion attempt and reacts to it automatically. That would block a Stuxnet-like virus as soon as it jumped from the USB stick. But how can an operating system know which programs are to be trusted?

One solution is to use a one-way hash function, a cryptographic technique. A hash function takes a fantastically huge number–for example, all the millions of 1s and 0s of a computer program, expressed as a number–and converts it to a much smaller number, which acts as a signature. Because programs are so large, it is highly unlikely that two different ones would result in the same signature value. Imagine that every program that wants to run on a system must first go through the hash function. Its signature then gets checked against a master list; if it does not check out, the attack stops there.

The doe also recommends other security measures, such as physical security checks at operator workstations (think radio chips in identification badges). It also highlights the need to exert tighter control over communication between devices inside the network.

The 2007 Aurora demonstration involved a rogue device tricking a generator's network into believing it was sending authoritative commands. These commands eventually led to the destruction of the generator.

These worthwhile steps will require time and money and effort. If we are going to achieve the doe roadmap to a more secure grid in the next decade, we are going to have to pick up the pace. Let us hope we have even that much time.

About the Author

David M. Nicol is director of the Information Trust Institute and a professor in the department of electrical and computer engineering at the University of Illinois at Urbana-Champaign. He has worked as a consultant for the U.S. Department of Homeland Security and Department of Energy.

Russia's Information War Is Being Waged on Social Media Platforms

By Sophie Bushwick

Days after Russia invaded Ukraine, multiple social media platforms–including Facebook, Twitter and YouTube–announced they had dismantled coordinated networks of accounts spreading disinformation. These networks, which were comprised of fabricated accounts disguised with fake names and AI-generated profile images or hacked accounts, were sharing suspiciously similar anti-Ukraine talking points, suggesting they were being controlled by centralized sources linked to Russia and Belarus.

Russia's Internet Research Agency used similar disinformation campaigns to amplify propaganda about the U.S. election in 2016. But their extent was unclear until after the election–and at the time, they were conducted with little pushback from social media platforms. "There was a sense that the platforms just didn't know what to do," says Laura Edelson, a misinformation researcher and Ph.D. candidate in computer science at New York University. Since then, she says, platforms and governments have become more adept at combating this type of information warfare–and more willing to deplatform bad actors that deliberately spread disinformation. Edelson spoke to *Scientific American* about how an information war is being waged as the conflict continues.

[An edited transcript of the interview follows.]

Q: How do social media platforms combat accounts that spread disinformation?

A: These kinds of disinformation campaigns–where they are specifically misleading users about the source of the content–that's really easy for platforms to take action against because Facebook has this real name policy: misleading users about who you are is a violation of Facebook's platform rules. But there are [other] things that shouldn't be difficult to take down—that historically Facebook has really struggled with—and that is actors like RT. RT is a Russian state-backed media outlet. And Facebook has really struggled historically on what to do with that. That's what was so impressive about seeing that [Facebook and other platforms] really did start to take some action against RT in the past week, because this has been going on for such a long time. And also, frankly, [social media platforms] have had cover from governments, where governments in Europe have banned Russian state media. And that has given cover to Facebook, YouTube and other major platforms to do the same thing. In general, banning anyone—but especially banning media—is not a step anyone should take lightly. But RT and Sputnik [another Russia state-backed media outlet] are not regular media: they have such a long track record of polluting the information space.

Q: What else can be done to fight harmful false information?

A: One of the things that the U.S. did really well going into this conflict—and why, at least from a misinformation [controlling] perspective, the first week went very well—is that the U.S. government was really aggressive with releasing information about what it knew about the ground realities in Russia and Ukraine. That was really helpful for creating a space where it was difficult for the Russians to put out misinformation about those same things. Because the U.S. government was very forthcoming, it didn't leave a lot of room; there wasn't an information vacuum that the Russians could step in and fill. And then the Ukrainian government has been tremendously savvy in telling the story of the Ukrainian resistance. There are definitely times when it has stepped over the line into propaganda. But in general, it has made sure that the world sees the Ukrainian resistance and the fight that the Ukrainian people are willing to put up. That [helps] people see what is going on and understand that the people who are there fighting are real people who, not that long ago, were not fighters. They were civilians, and now they are defending their country.

I think both of those things are going to be difficult to maintain over time. But if they are not maintained, then the window for Russian misinformation will open. A challenge we are all going to have to deal with is that this war is not going to be over in the next few days, but the news cycle cannot maintain this level of focus on these events. It's shocking to say, but in three weeks' time, you will have hours go by without thinking about it. And that is when people's guards are going to go down. If someone is trying to spread some kind of [disinformation]–maybe the Russians make up some fake Ukrainian atrocity or something–that's when the world is going to be susceptible to that kind of thing. And that's when we're going to have to remember all this stuff of "Who was telling you the story? Do we trust them? How verifiable is this account?" This is going to be part of how conflict is waged going forward. But this is something that is new for all actors, and everyone is going to have to get used to keeping up their ground game in the information war, not just in the kinetic war.

Q: Some people have also pointed out an apparent reduction in other forms of misinformation, such as vaccine-related conspiracy theories, since Russia's Internet infrastructure and payment networks were limited by sanctions. What is going on with that?

A: I haven't seen a large-scale analysis published about this. That said, there have been quite a few anecdotal reports that misinformation in other sectors has decreased markedly in the past week. We can't say for certain that this is because of lack of Internet access in Russia. The conclusion is not that all of this stuff that had been taken down was sourced from Russia. The conclusion that's reasonable to draw from these anecdotal reports is that Russian Internet infrastructure was a vital part of the tool kit of people who spread misinformation. There's a lot of pieces of this economy that are run out of Russia–bot networks, for example, networks of people who sell who buy and sell stolen credit card information, a lot of the economy around buying stolen [social media] accounts–because Russia has historically tolerated a lot of cybercrime. Either it turns a blind eye or a lot of these groups actually directly work for, or are contractors to, the Russian state.

Q: How can we avoid falling for or spreading misinformation?

A: The bottom line is that people shouldn't have to do this. This is kind of like saying, "My car doesn't have any seat belt. What can I do to protect myself in a crash?" The answer is: your car should have seat belts, and that shouldn't be your job. But unfortunately, it is. With that small caveat, you have to remember that the most successful misinformation succeeds by appealing to emotions rather than reason. If misinformation can tap into that emotive pathway, you're never going to question it because it feels good, and if it feels good, it's adjacent to being true. So the first thing that I recommend is: if something makes you feel emotional–particularly if something makes you feel angry–before you share it or interact with it, really ask yourself the question "Who is promoting this, and do I trust them?"

Q: What is the most important thing platforms need to do to install metaphorical seat belts?

A: I think the single biggest thing that platforms should be doing, especially in these moments of crisis, is [recognize they] should not promote content solely based on engagement. Because you have to remember that misinformation is really engaging. It is engaging because of some of those reasons I talked about: highly emotive appeal, things that circumvent reason and go straight to the gut. That's a really effective tactic for deception. So I think this is when platforms need to step up the importance of quality of content versus how engaging content is. That is the number one thing they could do, and almost everything else pales in comparison.

About the Author

Sophie Bushwick is an associate editor covering technology at Scientific American.

Russian Misinformation Seeks to Confound, Not Convince

By David Robert Grimes

As war envelops Ukraine, Russian sources have strived to create a miasma of disinformation about the invasion. Among ample efforts to distort reality, the Russian Ministry of Defense asserted recently that U.S.-backed labs in Ukraine have been developing bioweapons. Outlandish as this falsehood may be, Fox's Tucker Carlson gave it credence by arguing that the U.S. government's response was a "cover-up."

As the Russia-Ukraine war intensifies, so too will the flow of disinformation. This is an age-old strategy Russia has long history of employing, and a playbook that others, most notably anti-vaccine activists, have borrowed from liberally. Yet, rather than focusing effort on convincing people of a falsehood, the Russian strategy takes a tack reminiscent of a strategy long employed by the tobacco industry: to sow so much doubt about what is true that it sends people into decision paralysis. Faced with a cacophony of wild and conflicting claims, people do nothing, unsure of what is right.

Despite constituting only a small part of our media diet, disinformation campaigns, in our digital world, can be devastatingly effective. We are intrinsically biased towards information that is emotionally visceral. We afford more weight to content that frightens or outrages us, with the ability to induce anger serving as the single greatest predictor of whether content goes viral. This propels the most visceral, divisive narratives to the forefront of discourse, creating a sound and fury of passionately debated claims and counter claims. In that atmosphere, it becomes increasingly difficult to ascertain what to believe, and easy to abandon the task of discerning the truth.

If we are not to fall victim to such rank dishonesty, it is crucial now that we question our sources more carefully than ever before.

Indecision and distraction have long been central to Russia's *dezinformatsiya* (disinformation) policy, a term Stalin himself is credited with coining. While an ancient concept, Russia had by the imperial age mastered dark obfuscation techniques refined for the era of mass communication. By the dawn of the Soviet empire, they realized this potential on an industrial scale, establishing the world's first office dedicated to disinformation in 1923. In the 1960s, the KGB covertly sponsored American fringe groups, amplifying conspiratorial narratives about everything from the assassination of president John F. Kennedy to water fluoridation.

The goal, as KGB Major General Oleg Kalugin elucidated in 1998, was "not intelligence collection, but subversion: active measures to weaken the West, to drive wedges in the Western community alliances of all sorts, particularly NATO, to sow discord among allies, to weaken the United States in the eyes of the people of Europe, Asia, Africa, Latin America....". Operation INFEKTION, a mid-1980s clandestine effort to spread the myth that AIDS was a CIA-designed bioweapon, was but one infamous exemplar. While utterly fictious, it resonated with communities ravaged by HIV and neglected by the callous indifference of the Reagan administration. Despite Russian intelligence taking responsibility for this lie in 1992, the legacy of AIDS denialism persists to this day worldwide.

During the Cold War, the doctrine of "active measures" was the beating heart of Soviet intelligence. This philosophy of political and information warfare had wide remit, including front groups, media manipulation, counterfeiting, infiltrating peace groups and even the occasional assassination.

And in our media-saturated era, Russia has been, by far, disinformation's most enthusiastic user. Take the 2016 U.S. presidential election and the contentious Brexit referendum; Russia appears to have influenced both via lies and distortions.

But disinformation is not solely confined to geopolitics. By summer 2020, the European Commission identified a concerted Russian drive to propagate COVID disinformation worldwide. From the outset of the pandemic, Kremlin-backed troll farms pushed the narrative that COVID was an engineered bioweapon, peddling the explosive fiction that 5G radio frequencies caused the virus–a lie that resulted in dozens of arson attacks on cell towers worldwide.

There is a dark irony in the observation that conspiracy-minded people can be weaponized in plots to which they're entirely oblivious. The enduring popularity of the virus-as-a-bioweapon mantra is a stark reminder that in the age of social media, such manipulation has become ever easier and more effective. Perhaps the most odious example of this is the cynical rise of anti-vaccine propaganda.

The sheer efficacy of vaccination is scientifically incontrovertible, and after clean water, immunization is the most life-saving intervention in human history. Despite this, the last decade has witnessed precipitous drops in vaccine confidence worldwide. The renaissance of once-virtually-conquered diseases prompted the WHO to declare vaccine hesitancy a top-10 threat to public health in 2019.

Vaccine hesitancy is a spectrum rather than a simple binary, and exposure to anti-vaccine conspiracy theories nudges recipients towards rejection. But critically, many who decline vaccination are not dyed-in-the-wool anti-vaccine zealots, but simply scared by what they have heard, unsure what to believe. Our tendency towards the illusory truth effect exacerbates this inertia, as the mere repetition of a fiction is enough to prime us to accept it, even if we know it to be false on an intellectual level. While Russia has often amplified anti-vaccine conspiracy theories to increase tensions, the anti-vaccine movements exist independently of these efforts, and are masters at sowing the seeds of doubt with torrents of conflicting and emotive claims.

This illustrates the grim reality that disinformation has no need for consistency and zero commitment to objective reality; claims are frequently contradictory, arguing both sides of the coin in exaggerated and divisive ways. This "Russian firehose" model of propaganda is high-output, contradictory and multichannel. The stream encourages us to sleepwalk into apathy, distrustful of everything. This renders us supremely malleable, and dangerously disengaged.

When it comes to vaccination, concerned parents often opt to stay with the devil they know, delaying or even rejecting vaccination rather than sifting through the symphony of conflicting claims to which they're subjected. Similarly, the outpouring of fictions about Ukraine, its president, Volodymyr Zelensky, and the war is designed to overwhelm our capacity to analyze, inducing us to implicitly accept uncertainty over aggressor and aggrieved–a manufactured doubt benefitting Russia and other nations.

Conviction is not the chief goal of disinformation; instilling doubt is. This is why anti-vaccine activists have been so successful online, and why Russian troll-farms push ample resources into hawking lies virtually everywhere. The ubiquity of these fictions gives them an implicit veneer of legitimacy, fueling polarization and distrust.

This is the strategy Putin continues to pursue; already Russian propaganda has tried to paint Ukraine (or NATO / America) as aggressors with staged disinformation. This has been rendered less effective by the Biden administration's creative approach of releasing intelligence prior to the operation. Across social media, Russian front organizations still try to induce doubt, efforts that will only intensify as the war wages on. Truth, the old adage insists, is the first casualty of war.

About the Author

David Robert Grimes is a scientist and author of Good Thinking: Why Flawed Logic Puts Us All at Risk and How Critical Thinking Can Save the World *(The Experiment, 2021). His work focuses on health disinformation and conspiracy theory, and he is an international advocate for the public understanding of science. Grimes is a recipient of the* Nature*/Sense about Science Maddox Prize and a fellow of the Committee for Skeptical Inquiry.*

Section 2: War of the Machines

War of the Machines: A Dramatic Growth in the Military Use of Robots Brings Evolution in Their Conception

By P. W. Singer

Back in the early 1970s, a handful of scientists, engineers, defense contractors and U.S. Air Force officers got together to form a professional group. They were essentially trying to solve the same problem: how to build machines that can operate on their own without human control and to figure out ways to convince both the public and a reluctant Pentagon brass that robots on the battlefield are a good idea. For decades they met once or twice a year, in relative obscurity, to talk over technical issues, exchange gossip and renew old friendships. This once cozy group, the Association for Unmanned Systems International, now encompasses more than 1,500 member companies and organizations from 55 countries. The growth happened so fast, in fact, that it found itself in something of an identity crisis. At one of its meetings in San Diego, it even hired a "master storyteller" to help the group pull together the narrative of the amazing changes in robotic technology. As one attendee summed up, "Where have we come from? Where are we? And where should we–and where do we want to–go?"

What prompted the group's soul-searching is one of the most profound changes in modern warfare since the advent of gunpowder or the airplane: an astonishingly rapid rise in the use of robots on the battlefield. Not a single robot accompanied the U.S. advance from Kuwait toward Baghdad in 2003. Since then, 7,000 "unmanned" aircraft and another 12,000 ground vehicles have entered the U.S. military inventory, entrusted with missions that range from seeking out snipers to bombing the hideouts of al-Qaeda higher-ups in Pakistan. The world's most powerful fighting forces, which once eschewed robots as unbecoming to their warrior culture, have now embraced a war of the machines as a means of combating an irregular enemy that triggers remote explosions with cell phones and then blends back into the crowd. These robotic systems are not only having a big effect on how this new type of warfare is fought, but they also have initiated a set of contentious arguments about the implications of using ever more autonomous and intelligent machines in battle. Moving soldiers out of harm's way may save lives, but the growing use of robots also raises deep political, legal and ethical questions about the fundamental nature of warfare and whether these technologies could inadvertently make wars easier to start.

The earliest threads of this story arguably hark back to the 1921 play *R.U.R.*, in which Czech writer Karel Čapek coined the word "robot" to describe mechanical servants that eventually rise up against their human masters. The word was packed with meaning, because it derived from the Czech word for "servitude" and the older Slavic word for "slave," historically linked to the "robotniks," peasants who had revolted against rich landowners in the 1800s. This theme of robots taking on the work we don't want to do but then ultimately assuming control is a staple of science fiction that continues today in *The Terminator* and *The Matrix*.

Today roboticists invoke the descriptors "unmanned" or "remote-operated" to avoid Hollywood-fueled visions of machines that are plotting our demise. In the simplest terms, robots are machines built to operate in a "sense-think-act" paradigm. That is, they have sensors that gather information about the world. Those data are then relayed to computer processors, and perhaps artificial-intelligence software, that use them to make appropriate decisions. Finally, based on that information, mechanical systems known as effectors carry out some physical action on the world around them. Robots do not have to be anthropomorphic, as is the other Hollywood trope of a man in a metal suit. The size and shape of the systems that are beginning to carry out these actions vary widely and rarely evoke the image of C-3PO or the Terminator.

The Global Positioning Satellite system, video-game-like remote controls and a host of other technologies have made robots both useful and usable on the battlefield during the past decade. The increased ability to observe, pinpoint and then attack targets in hostile settings without having to expose the human operator to danger became a priority after the 9/11 attacks, and each new use of the systems on the ground created a success story that had broader repercussions. As an example, in the first few months of the Afghan campaign in 2001, a prototype of the PackBot, now used extensively to defuse bombs, was sent into the field for testing. The soldiers liked it so much that they would not return it to its manufacturer, iRobot, which has since gone on to sell thousands. Similarly, another robotics company executive recounts that before 9/11, he could not get his calls returned by the Pentagon. Afterward, he was told: "Make 'em as fast as you can."

This accelerating acceptance of military robotics became apparent as the Iraq War played out. When U.S. forces went into Iraq in 2003, the ground invasion force had no unmanned systems. By the end of 2004 the number had risen to 150 or so. A year later it had reached 2,400. Today the overall U.S. military inventory is more than 12,000. The same trend occurred with air weaponry: the U.S. military went from having a handful of unmanned aerial vehicles supporting the invasion force to more than 7,000 now. And this progression is just the start. One U.S. Air Force three-star general forecasts that the next major U.S. conflict will involve not the thousands of robots currently in the field but "tens of thousands."

The raw numbers reveal an important shift in attitude by a military that just a few years ago remained dubious of its capabilities and protective of the age-old warrior's prerogative of leading the charge into combat. Today the U.S. Air Force, Army and Navy entice teenage recruits through television advertising that extols how, as one promotion puts it, the U.S. Navy is "working every day to unman the front lines."

When teens do join the military, exposure to automated systems is integral to their experience, from induction to discharge. They use the latest virtual-training software to learn how to operate a particular weapons system. After training, they may well operate a lawnmower-size PackBot or a TALON ground robot that can defuse bombs or peek over the top of a ridge in the hunt for insurgents in Iraq or Afghanistan.

If they end up at sea, they may well serve on an Aegis-class destroyer or Littoral Combat Ship, which operate as mother ships for a range of systems, from Fire Scout unmanned helicopters to Protector robotic sentry motorboats. If their career takes them into submarines, they could end up controlling unmanned underwater vehicles such as the REMUS (Remote Environmental Monitoring Units, a torpedo-shaped robot sub originally developed by the Woods Hole Oceanographic Institution) to detect mines or to conduct surveillance of unfriendly coastlines. If they become aviators, they may "fly" Predator or Global Hawk drones over Central Asia, while never physically leaving the continental U.S.

The War Bots of Tomorrow

Such technologies are billed in a recruiting ad as part of today's military, while "seeming like science fiction." In reality, they are merely the first generation, a suggestion of more to come. That is, today's PackBot robot hunting roadside bombs and the Predator drones flying over Afghanistan represent the equivalent of the Model T Ford and the Wright brothers' Flyer. Prototypes for the next generation reveal three key ways that robots will change how we conduct warfare.

The idea of robots as mere "unmanned systems"–identical to any other machine, except without the presence of a human operator inside–is beginning to fade. The evolution recapitulates the trajectory of automotive history: thinking about cars as mere "horseless carriages" became an artifact as designers started to consider wholly novel forms and sizes. The similar casting off of preconceptions about robots is leading the machines to take on a wide range of shapes. As would be expected, some models take their inspiration from biology. Boston Dynamics's BigDog, for one, is a metallic, equipment-toting quadruped. Others are hybrids, such as a Naval Postgraduate School surveillance bot that has both wings and legs. But other systems in early development have literally no form at all. ChemBot, a creation of the University of Chicago and iRobot, is a bloblike machine that shifts shape, such that it is able to squeeze through a hole in the wall.

With no humans inside, the size of robots can range wildly. Miniaturized robots already measure in millimeters and weigh in grams. Take a surveillance bot made by AeroVironment for urban combat. It mimics a hummingbird in size and in its ability to hover over a target. The next frontier is nanoscale robotics (structures measured in billionths of a meter) that some scientists believe will become commonplace within a few decades. In war these machines might be used for roles that range from "smart dust" that detects the enemy to cellular-level machines inside the human body that repair wounds or, in turn, cause them. At the other end of the scale, the ability to deploy a system that does not have to take into account human bodily needs is leading to gigantic unmanned systems, such as Lockheed Martin's High-Altitude Airship, an unmanned blimp that carries a radar the length of a football field, designed to fly at above 19,800 meters for more than a month at a time.

Beyond size and shape, a second key change is the widening of roles these machines can perform in warfare. Much like the early "aeroplanes" in World War I, robots started out only for observation and reconnaissance and have now expanded into new tasks. Technology development company QinetiQ North America, maker of the TALON, introduced the MAARS robot in 2007, which is armed with a machine gun and grenade launcher and can take on sentry and sniper duty. In turn, med bots such as the U.S. Army Medical Research and Materiel Command's Robotic Extraction Vehicle are designed to drag wounded soldiers to safety and then administer care.

The third key change is the robots' ever growing intelligence and autonomy. The inexorable growth in computing power means that today's recently enlisted soldiers may end their careers witnessing robots powered by computers literally a billion times more capable than those currently available. The World War II–era military did not differentiate between the B-17 and B-24 bomber by how smart they were, but latter-day weapons systems require just such distinctions. The Predator series of unmanned planes, for example, has evolved from being purely remote-controlled to now being able to take off and land on their own and track 12 targets at once; the target-recognition software can even trace footprints back to their point of origin. Even so, the U.S. military is already planning to replace these planes, deployed since 1995, with a newer generation.

The expansion of robotic intelligence and autonomy raises profound questions of what roles are appropriate to outsource to machines. These decisions must be weighed on how effective the machines might be in battle but also on what this shift in responsibility would mean for both their human commanders and broader political, ethical and legal responsibility for their conduct. The most likely outcome in the near future is for robots to take on the semblance of "war fighter associates." In this scenario, mixed teams of humans and robots would work together, each doing what they do best. The human element may well turn out to be akin to the quarterback in a football game, calling plays for robotic teammates, while giving them enough autonomy to react to changing circumstances.

The Real Story

These remarkable developments may still not fully capture the story of where robotics is headed and what it means for our world and the future of warfare. The full implications cannot be gleaned from describing physical capabilities, just as the significance of gunpowder is not captured by noting that it produced a chemical explosion that allowed a longer trajectory for projectiles.

Robots are one of those rare inventions that literally change the rules of the game. Such a "revolutionary" technology does not give one side a permanent advantage, as some analysts mistakenly believe, because it is quickly adopted by or adapted to by other combatants.

Rather it causes shake-ups, not only on the battlefield but in the social structures surrounding it. The longbow, for example, was not notable simply because it allowed the English to beat the French at the Battle of Agincourt during the Hundred Years' War; rather it let organized groups of peasants triumph over knights, ending the age of feudalism.

An apt historical parallel to the current period may well turn out to be World War I. Back then, strange, exciting new technologies that had been viewed as merely science fiction just years earlier were introduced and then used in increasing numbers on the battlefield. Indeed, it was H. G. Wells's 1903 short story "Land Ironclads" that inspired Winston Churchill, then First Lord of the Admiralty, to champion the development of the tank. Another story, by A. A. Milne, creator of the beloved *Winnie-the-Pooh* series, was among the first to raise the idea of using airplanes in war, while Arthur Conan Doyle (in his 1914 short story "Danger!") and Jules Verne (in his 1869 novel *20,000 Leagues under the Sea*) pioneered the notion of submarines' full use in war. First users had an edge, but it was fleeting. British invention and early exploitation of tanks in World War I, for example, was surmounted a mere 20 years later when the Germans proved with their blitzkrieg tactics that they had figured out how to use the new weapon more effectively.

The arrival of tanks, airplanes and submarines was important, however, because they raised a wholly new set of political, moral and legal issues that resulted in dramatic strategic consequences. For instance, differing interpretations between the U.S. and Germany over how submarines were legally allowed to fight (should they be allowed to sink merchant ships without warning?) drew America into the First World War, ultimately leading to its rise to superpower status. Similarly, airplanes proved useful not only at spotting and attacking troops at greater distances, but also at allowing the emergence of aerial bombing that often resulted in bombs raining onto civilian populations, giving an entirely new meaning to the term "home front."

The Plot Thickens

We are seeing much the same circumstances today with military robotics. Take the idea of what it once meant to "go to war." For democratic nations, it long signified a serious commitment that involved currying public favor for an endeavor that jeopardized not just the lives of its citizens' sons and daughters but the state's very survival. Unmanned systems (and their ability to carry out remote acts of force) erode the deterrent exerted by public sentiment, a decline already begun by the end of the U.S. military draft in 1979.

This distancing of the human combatant from the theater of conflict may well make wars easier to start and may even change how we view them. For example, the U.S. has carried out more than 130 air strikes into Pakistan using Predator and Reaper unmanned craft. This number is more than triple the total of manned bomber strikes that we launched in the opening round of the Kosovo War a mere decade ago. But unlike that war, robotic air strikes into Pakistan prompted no debate at all in Congress and relatively little reporting in the media. In essence, we are engaging in what we would have previously called a "war," but without public deliberation. The conflict is not even considered a war, because it comes without any cost in U.S. human lives. By one measure, these strikes have been highly effective. They have killed as many as 40 leaders of al-Qaeda, the Taliban and allied militant groups without having to send American troops or pilots into harm's way. But the repercussions of these strikes raise questions that are still being answered.

What is, for one, this technology's impact on the "war of ideas" we are fighting against terrorist recruiting and propaganda? That is, how and why is the reality of our painstaking efforts to act with precision emerging on the other side of the globe through a cloud of anger and misperception? Whereas we use adjectives such as "precise" and "costless" to describe the technology in our mass media, a leading newspaper in Pakistan declared the U.S. to be a "principal hate figure" and "all-purpose scapegoat" because of the strikes. Unfortunately, "drone" has become a colloquial word in Urdu, appearing in rock lyrics that accuse America of not fighting with honor. This issue becomes more complex when weighing who should be held accountable when things go wrong. Estimates of civilian casualties range from 200 to 1,000. But many of these incidents occurred close to some of the most dangerous terrorist leaders around. Where does one draw the line?

The meaning of "going to war" is also changing for the individual warrior in 2010. Setting off to battle has always meant that a soldier might never come home. Achilles and Odysseus sailed off to fight Troy. My grandfather shipped out to fight the Japanese after Pearl Harbor. Remote warfare has changed the enduring truth of the past 5,000 years of war. A growing number of soldiers wake up, drive to work, sit in front of computers and use robotic systems to battle insurgents 11,300 kilometers away. At the end of a day "at war," they get back in their cars, drive home and, as one U.S. Air Force officer put it: "Within 20 minutes you are sitting at the dinner table talking to your kids." The most dangerous part of their day is not the dangers of the battlefield but the commute home.

This disconnection from the battlefield also leads to a demographic change in who does what in war and the issues it provokes about a soldier's identity (young enlisted troops doing jobs once limited to senior officers) or status (the technician versus the warrior) or the nature of combat stress and fatigue. Remote operators may seem like they are just playing video games, but they experience a psychological burden of fighting day after day after day, with lives on the ground depending on their flawless performance. Their commanders describe the challenges of leading units fighting remotely as being far different and sometimes even more difficult than leading regular units physically in battle.

With each step in the growing lethality and intelligence of robotics, the role of the "man in the loop" of decision making in war has begun to diminish. For example, the pace of war is such that only systems such as the Counter-Rocket Artillery and

Mortar, or C-RAM (which looks a bit like the *Star Wars* robot R2-D2, with a 20-millimeter automatic machine gun attached) can react quickly enough to shoot down incoming rockets or missiles. The human is certainly part of the decision making but mainly in the initial programming of the robot. During the actual operation of the machine, the operator really only exercises veto power, and a decision to override a robot's decision must be made in only half a second, with few willing to challenge what they view as the better judgment of the machine.

Many observers argue that such a trend will lower the likely mistakes in war, as well as ensure that the laws of war are uniformly followed, as if they were software code in a computer processor. Yet this attitude ignores the complex environment of war. An unmanned system may be able to pick out a man carrying an AK-47 rifle from over a kilometer away and tell whether he fired it recently or not (by the weapon's thermal signature), but knowing whether that man is an insurgent, a member of an allied militia or a simple shopkeeper will be as hard for the machine as it is today for any human soldier.

Nor is the age-old "fog of war" being lifted by technology, as former defense secretary Donald H. Rumsfeld and other advocates for the digital battlefield once believed. For instance, the sophisticated C-RAM technology reportedly once mistook a U.S. Army helicopter for an enemy target because of a programming error. Fortunately, no one was hurt. Unluckily, what an investigative report described as a "software glitch" in a similar antiaircraft system in South Africa produced a less benign outcome in 2007. Armed with a 35-millimeter cannon, the weapon was supposed to fire into the sky during a training exercise. Instead it leveled and fired in a circle, killing nine soldiers before it ran out of ammunition.

Such incidents, of course, raise immense legal concerns. How should one apportion accountability? What system of law can even be relied on for guidance? These instances demonstrate that technology often moves faster than our social institutions. How do we reconcile our 20th-century laws of war to the new reality?

A New Beginning

Our definitions and understandings of war, how it is fought and even who should fight are in great flux, driven by a remarkable new technology that delivers immense capability. Humankind has been in this same kind of situation before. We often struggle to integrate and understand new technologies and then eventually look at what was once considered strange and even unacceptable as completely normal. Perhaps the best example can be invoked from the 1400s, when one French nobleman argued that guns were tools of murder a true soldier would not deign to use. Only cowards, he wrote, "would not dare to look in the face of the men they bring down from a distance with their wretched bullets."

We have "progressed" since then, but the story today is much the same with robotics. Mastery of the technology may turn out to be much easier to address than the policy dilemmas arising from the incredible capabilities of machines that can change the world around them. Indeed, it is for this reason that some scientists invoke a different historic parallel to where we stand now with robotics than the gun or airplane, instead citing the atomic bomb. We are creating an exciting technology that is pushing the frontiers of science but raises such penetrating concerns beyond the scientific realm that we may well come to regret these elaborate engineering creations, as did some designers of early nuclear warheads. Of course, just like those inventors back in the 1940s, today's robotics developers continue their work because it is militarily useful, highly profitable, as well as the cutting edge of science. As Albert Einstein supposedly said, "If we knew what it was we were doing, it would not be called research, would it?"

The real story is that what was once only fodder for science-fiction conventions has to be discussed seriously and not only at the Pentagon. This narrative is of importance not solely to what takes place at robotic trade group meetings, in the research labs or on the battlefield but to how the overall tale of humanity is playing itself out. Humankind had a 5,000-year monopoly on the fighting of war. That monopoly has ended.

About the Author

P. W. Singer directs the 21st Century Defense Initiative at the Brookings Institution and is author of the best-selling 2009 book Wired for War: The Robotics Revolution and Conflict in the 21st Century.

The Drone Wars: 9/11-Inspired Combat Leans Heavily on Robot Aircraft

By Larry Greenemeier

The September 11, 2001 attacks initiated a flurry of advances in military technology over the past decade that has helped the U.S. and its allies redefine modern warfare. None of these advancements have had a greater impact on America's missions in the Middle East than the maturation of remotely piloted aircraft (RPA), also known as unmanned aerial vehicles (UAVs) or, more generically, drones. The U.S. Army's drone armada alone has expanded from 54 drones in October 2001, when U.S. combat operations began in Afghanistan, to more than 4,000 drones performing surveillance, reconnaissance and attack missions in Afghanistan, Iraq and Pakistan. There are more than 6,000 of them throughout the U.S. military as a whole, and continued developments promise to make these controversial aircraft–blamed for the deaths of militants as well as citizens–far more intelligent and nimble.

Whereas drones themselves are certainly not a new concept–their origins can be traced back to the 1840s–since 9/11 they can now be loaded with a variety of sensors and weapons and are controlled by highly trained operators using a joystick and video monitor thousands of kilometers from a combat zone.

"One of the most significant things that has occurred since 9/11 is the shift from, if you will, peer-to-peer warfare to a focus on irregular warfare," says U.S. Air Force chief scientist Mark Maybury. RPAs, as the Air Force refers to them because they are indeed operated by pilots, are helping U.S. troops and their allies adjust to that shift by delivering reconnaissance data and attack support against enemies difficult to spot because of their ability to blend in with noncombatants and the rugged terrain of their surroundings.

Use of drones has grown across several branches of the military as well as the CIA (one of the earliest users of unmanned aircraft).

The Air Force, for example, logged its first 250,000 hours of drone flight time between 1995 and May 2007. The next 250,000 hours of drone flight time, however, took only a year and a half, from May 2007 to November 2008. The Air Force achieved its third set of 250,000 flight-time hours in just one year, from December 2008 to December 2009.

The Department of Defense's 2012 plan calls for "purchasing more of the existing unmanned aircraft systems for current operations, improving the systems already in service, and designing more-capable unmanned aircraft systems for the future," according to a Congressional Budget Office (CBO) report published in June. The CBO estimates that the Defense Department will spend about $36.9 billion across its different branches on 730 new medium-sized and large drones through 2020.

This expansion of the military's unmanned aircraft campaign brings with it a degree of concern as drones have come under fire by critics. Some dispute the military's accuracy claims and point to unmanned aircraft as the cause of thousands of civilian deaths in the war-torn Middle East over the past decade. Others note that the fight against terrorist organizations such as al Qaeda embedded in civilian zones–most notably the killing of Osama bin Laden–has primarily been carried out using time-tested intelligence methods rather than drone-launched Hellfire air-to-surface missiles.

Dawn of the Drone

The use of unmanned aircraft in war goes back 162 years, when Austria used pilotless balloons to drop bombs on Venice in 1849. As *Scientific American* reported at the time: "In a favorable wind the balloons will be launched and directed as near to Venice as possible, and on their being brought to vertical positions over the town, they will be fired by electro magnetism by means of a long isolated copper wire with a large galvanic battery placed on the shore. The bomb falls perpendicularly, and explodes on reaching the ground."

In the early 20th century the U.S. military recruited remote-controlled airplanes to serve as decoys or even to attack enemy targets during the First and Second World wars. From the 1950s, these aircraft began to support troops with the aid of cameras, sensors, communications equipment or other payloads. "In terms of modern use, drones really started in the early 1990s, where they were an advanced concept technology demonstration at DARPA [the Defense Advanced Research Projects Agency]," Maybury adds.

General Atomics Aeronautical Systems, Inc.'s Predator drones were introduced to combat in the mid-1990s and deployed in the U.S.'s 1999 Kosovo air campaign for surveillance and reconnaissance. Predators (which have a 20-meter wingspan) were first used in Afghanistan in October 2001 to provide intelligence and a strike capability to Operation Enduring Freedom, the official name used by the U.S. government for the war in Afghanistan. A CIA-controlled Predator drone firing a Hellfire missile killed six suspected al Qaeda terrorists in Yemen on November 3, 2002–the first use of an armed Predator as an attack aircraft outside of a theater of war such as Afghanistan, according to the Federation of American Scientists (FAS).

Stepping Up Drone Missions

In the past year alone, the Air Force has supported more than 400 firefights involving RPAs, Maybury says. In 2010 they captured 30,000 hours of full motion video during their missions along with 11,000 high fidelity images. "We call them remotely piloted aircraft because in fact we have professionals–both pilots and sensor operators–operating them," Maybury says. "I don't even like the word 'drones.' It sounds boring personally."

The Air Force's large-scale RPA deployment began after 9/11; it had a single RPA in operation in 2001. The Air Force now operates at least four different models of medium-sized or large unmanned aircraft. In addition to its 175 Predators, there are 14 jet-powered Northrop Grumman RQ-4 Global Hawks, the largest RPAs in the Air

Force's fleet with wingspans of 35 to 40 meters. About 40 turboprop-powered General Atomics MQ-9 Reapers (a larger version of the Predator) were supposed to be entering the fleet this year. The Air Force also uses the Lockheed Martin RQ-170 Sentinel, a "stealthy reconnaissance aircraft whose existence has only recently been acknowledged by the Air Force," the CBO reports.

Last year, for the first time in its history, the Air Force trained more RPA pilots than fixed-wing pilots. RPAs are often equipped with full-motion cameras, infrared cameras to provide night vision, signals intelligence sensors to eavesdrop on communications and a variety of other sensors. In addition to a pilot, each RPA has a sensor operator who directs the cameras and signals sensors during a mission. All of this information is fed to a system of "exploiters," Air Force personnel who analyze all of that streaming video and other signal intelligence coming in and feed information as needed back to the pilot and sensor operator.

Other branches of the military, as well as the CIA, have also come to rely heavily on drones. The Army primarily operates three medium-sized models of unmanned aircraft–Northrop Grumman MQ-5B Hunters, AAI Corp. RQ-7 Shadows (also used by the Marines), and two different types of Predators. The CBO estimates that the Army alone will spend about $5.9 billion in the next five years to add to its drone fleet.

The Navy is testing two new types of RPA–the long-endurance Broad Area Maritime Surveillance (BAMS) aircraft–a Global Hawk variant–and the Northrop Grumman MQ-8B Firescout unmanned helicopter. The Navy's plans call for purchasing 65 BAMS through 2026 and 168 Firescouts through 2028, according to the CBO.

ROVER Ground Stations

This wide variety of drones enables attacks on a diversity of enemy positions, but perhaps as significant is the ability to communicate with troops on the ground. This is done with the help of Remotely Operated Video Enhanced Receiver (ROVER) ground stations that combine a ruggedized laptop, software, a handset and a radio to give troops live, overhead intelligence from a variety of platforms—manned aircraft, unmanned aircraft, just about anything with a camera able to stream a data feed, says Chris Bronk, an information technology policy research fellow at Rice University's James A. Baker III Institute for Public Policy in Houston and a former U.S. State Department diplomat. "This helps American soldiers see beyond the next hill, in real time," he adds. The original ROVER system, developed in 2002, required a Humvee to lug it around. Newer systems can fit into a backpack.

ROVERs "are particularly transformational because now you have people on the ground who can see what the aircraft is seeing in the air in real time while also communicating with the DCGS [distributed common ground station] back in the U.S.," Maybury says. Troops with ROVERs can even request that RPA pilots and sensor operators fly or scan in a particular direction or over a particular area.

A key development in RPA operation over the past five years has been the ability to install systems of multiple cameras such as the Gorgon Stare video capture system and the Autonomous Real-time Ground Ubiquitous Surveillance Imaging System (ARGUS-IS). "Now we're able to see not just a single full-motion video but actually wide area motion imagery [WAMI], which provides multi-spot infrared imagery," Maybury says. "Ten years ago, you get a single feed, today we're looking at 65 spots of two frames a second around a wide area." A ROVER can dial into a particular channel or tell a sensor operator to follow a particular vehicle on a particular channel.

Micro Air Vehicles

Military and intelligence units have become increasingly interested in smaller drones that can improve reconnaissance and surveillance operations. Some of these drones are hand launched while others are even smaller and resemble birds and insects.

The Air Force Research Laboratory Air Vehicles Directorate Micro Air Vehicle Integration & Application Research Institute at Wright-Patterson Air Force Base in Ohio is dedicated to the development and testing of micro air vehicles (MAVs). Less than 0.6 meters in length, a MAV is capable of operating below rooftop level in an urban environment. It may have a fixed wing, rotary wing (helicopter), flapping wing or even no wings. The Air Force has been developing MAVs as a way of getting in close on enemy fighters, although such small devices are difficult to control (even a wind gust can take them out of position).

AeroVironment, Inc. is developing even smaller drones that weigh less than 20 grams. DARPA contracted the Monrovia, Calif., company to design and build a flying prototype "hummingbird-like" aircraft for the Nano Air Vehicle (NAV) program. In February AeroVironment introduced its 16-centimeter-long Nano Hummingbird, capable of climbing and descending vertically, flying sideways left and right, flying forward and backward, as well as rotating clockwise and counter-clockwise under remote control and carrying a small video camera.

The biologically inspired prototype is in the second phase of a three-phase DARPA NAV program, started in 2005. AeroVironment is one of four companies with phase-one contracts to develop miniature drones. The Charles Stark Draper Laboratory, Inc., in Cambridge, Mass., and Lockheed Martin have built rotary-wing NAVs, while AeroVironment and Oakland, Calif.,-based MicroPropulsion Corp. focused on flapping-wing aircraft.

Collateral Damage

Drones are promoted to the American public as a way to strike against threats to the U.S. without putting airmen or soldiers in harm's way. Another purported benefit of drones is the precision with which they attack America's enemies. Numerous reports of civilian casualties, however, indicate that these robotic aircraft are precise only to a certain degree. The CIA and White House have been quick to point out they have found no evidence of collateral deaths from U.S. counterterrorism operations outside of Afghanistan or Iraq, a claim disputed on several fronts, most recently in a report compiled by British and Pakistani journalists.

Reports of the number of civilian deaths attributed drone strikes vary, particularly in Pakistan. *The Long War Journal*, a Web site produced by nonprofit Public Multimedia Inc., claims that, since 2006 in Pakistan alone, drone strikes have killed 2,080 leaders and operatives from Taliban, al Qaeda, and allied extremist groups as well as 138 civilians. Meanwhile, the U.S. government claims that its drones have killed more than 2,000 militants in Pakistan and about 50 noncombatants since 2001. The Bureau of Investigative Journalism, a not-for-profit organization based at City University in London, disputes the U.S. government statistics, saying its research concluded that of the 2,292 people killed in U.S. attacks since 2004, 385 were civilians, including more than 160 children.

In an August 14 *New York Times* editorial, former director of national intelligence Dennis Blair, a retired admiral, pointed out that, particularly in Pakistan, "drone strikes are no longer the most effective strategy for eliminating al Qaeda's ability to attack us." His reasoning: "Drone strikes hinder Qaeda fighters while they move and hide, but they can endure the attacks and continue to function." In the meantime civilian casualties from drone strikes discourage support within Pakistan for the U.S.'s efforts to eliminate al Qaeda from that region, he wrote. Blair, however, does not call for an end to drone strikes but rather closer coordination between the U.S. and Pakistan militaries when planning such strikes.

The Future

One of the U.S. military's goals is to increase the use of drones on a variety of mission types. In addition to adding MAVs and NAVs to the mix, Maybury sees Air Force RPAs delivering fuel and other supplies to troops in the field. RPAs will also become increasingly autonomous, monitored but not necessarily piloted by humans. This will not be easy as autonomous systems must have the capability to adapt to changing conditions with the help of artificial intelligence that aids in decision making. Still, a long-term goal is to create fleets of RPAs that can travel as a self-coordinated unit and strike in concert. The Air Force claims it will build in override controls that enable pilots on the ground to reassign or reroute RPAs if necessary.

Missions for unmanned aircraft systems are expected to expand from reconnaissance and attacking ground targets to a much wider array of missions, including personnel recovery, airborne refueling, medical evacuation, and missile defense, according to FAS.

In addition to launching missiles, future drones may someday be able to fire directed energy weapons, including lasers to disrupt or destroy enemy equipment and high-power millimeter-wave systems designed to burn enemy combatants without being lethal.

Drones will also be able to stay in the air for years, rather than hours or days, at a time. "Last year, we did a lot of work in energy, which includes ultra-long endurance aircraft such as the Vulture and Integrated Sensor Is the Structure (ISIS), which are powered in part by lightweight solar cells," Maybury says.

Regardless of how far drone technology advances it is clear that the utility they have demonstrated in supporting U.S. troops over the past 10 years will ensure that these remotely controlled aircraft are here to stay.

About the Author

Larry Greenemeier is the associate editor of technology for Scientific American, *covering a variety of tech-related topics, including biotech, computers, military tech, nanotech and robots.*

Terminate the Terminators

By The Editors

When U.S. forces invaded Iraq in 2003, they fought a traditional war of human on human. Since then, robots have joined the fight. Both there and in Afghanistan, thousands of "unmanned" systems dismantle roadside IEDs, take that first peek around the corner at a sniper's lair and launch missiles at Taliban hideouts. Robots are pouring onto battlefields as if a new species of mechanotronic alien had just landed on our planet.

It is not the first time that the technology of warfare has advanced more rapidly than the body of international law that seeks to restrain its use. During World War I, cannons shot chemical weapons at and airplanes dropped bombs on unsuspecting cities. Only later did nations reach a verdict on whether it was acceptable to target a munitions factory next to a primary school.

Something similar is happening today with potentially even more profound and disturbing consequences. As Brookings Institution analyst P. W. Singer describes in "War of the Machines," the rise of robots leads to the frightening prospect of making obsolete the rule book by which nations go to war. Armed conflict between nation states is brutal, but at least it proceeds according to a set of rules grounded both in international law and in the demands of military discipline. It is not true that anything goes in the heat of battle. "Such rules are certainly not always followed, but their very existence is what separates killing in war from murder and what distinguishes soldiers from criminals," writes Singer in *Wired for War*, his recent popular book on the military robotic revolution.

Those rules are stretched to their breaking point when robots go to war. The legal and ethical questions abound. Who is accountable when a Predator's missile hits the wrong target? Missiles from errant drones have already killed as many as 1,000 civilians in Iraq, Afghanistan and Pakistan. Does responsibility reside with a field commander in the Middle East where spotters identified the "target of interest"? Or should blame be apportioned to the "remote pilot" stationed at a military base near Las Vegas who launched the strike from 7,000 miles away? And what about a software engineer who might have committed a programming error that caused a misfire?

Considering rules of engagement for war-at-a-distance raises a surreal set of questions. Does the remote operator in Nevada remain a legal combatant–in other words, a legitimate enemy target–on the trip after work to Walmart or to a daughter's soccer match? Would an increasingly sketchy line between warrior and civilian invite attacks on U.S. soil against homes and schools?

Remote-controlled robots are here to stay, and rules can be worked out to regulate their use. But the more serious threat comes from semiautonomous machines over which humans retain nothing more than last-ditch veto power. These systems are only a software upgrade away from fully self-sufficient operation. The prospect of androids that hunt down and kill on their own accord (shades of Terminator) should give us all pause. An automatic pilot that makes its own calls about whom to shoot violates the "human" part of international humanitarian law, the one that recognizes that some weapons are so abhorrent that they just should be eliminated.

Some might call a ban on autonomous robots naive or complain that it would tie the hands of soldiers faced with irregular warfare. But although robots have clear tactical advantages, they carry a heavy strategic price. The laws of war are an act not of charity but of self-interest; the U.S. would be weakened, not strengthened, if chemical and biological weapons were widespread, and the same is true of robots. They are a cheap way to offset conventional military strength, and other nations and groups such as Hezbollah in Lebanon are already deploying them. The U.S. may not always be the leader in this technology and would be well advised to negotiate restrictions on their use from a position of strength. We can never put the genie back into the bottle, but putting a hold on further development of this technology could limit the damage.

The organization best placed to work toward a ban is the International Committee of the Red Cross, the guardian of the

Geneva Conventions. A good starting point would be to convene a summit to consider armed, autonomous robots in the same framework as chemical and biological agents. The scientific community at large should get involved with this issue much as the Pugwash movement has worked toward nuclear arms control. Now is the time to take steps to ensure that a war of the machines remains nothing more than a science-fiction nightmare.

Are Cyborg Warriors a Good Idea?

By John Horgan

You already have a lot to worry about. Climate change, fake news, inequality, the stability of democracy. But I feel obliged to point out yet another threat: soldiers whose capabilities are enhanced by electronic devices implanted in their brains. Call them cyborg warriors.

Science fiction has been warning about cyborg warriors for a long time, mainstream journalism not so much. But several recent articles have focused on this potential peril, including one in *The Atlantic* titled "The Pentagon Wants to Weaponize the Brain." The subtitle asks, "What Could Go Wrong?"

Journalist Michael Joseph Gross reports on efforts of the Pentagon's think tank, the Defense Advanced Research Projects Agency, to create technologies that result in "merging minds and machines." The most dramatic are brain chips, arrays of electrodes that, when implanted in the brain, can receive electrical signals from and send them to neural tissue.

Officially, Darpa intends brain chips to help paralyzed and otherwise disabled veterans–for example, by allowing them to control computers and robotic limbs. Darpa is also interested in upgrading healthy soldiers, according to Gross. "What the agency learns from healing makes way for enhancement," he writes. "The mission is to make human beings something other than what we are, with powers beyond the ones we're born with and beyond ones we can organically attain."

In principle, brain chips could boost soldiers' cognitive and physical functions. Soldiers could control complex weapons systems with their thoughts, communicate telepathically with other soldiers and upload large databases instantly, like Neo in *The Matrix*. Minds containing brain chips can also be read and controlled by others. Again, in principle.

Gross cautions that "when scientists put electrodes in the brain, those devices eventually fail–after a few months or a few years." He quotes a neural engineer asserting that an implanted memory prosthesis, which requires understanding how the brain encodes complex information, is "far out of reach right now."

Like Gross, Raffi Khatchadourian, writing in *The New Yorker*, points out the limits as well as potential of brain-machine interfaces. Khatchadourian focuses on the work of a leading brain-implant researcher, Andrew Schwartz. In 2012 one of Schwartz's implant patients, Jan Scheuermann, who was paralyzed by a neurodegenerative disorder, fulfilled a fantasy, eating a chocolate bar with a robotic arm controlled by her thoughts. (Gross also describes Scheuermann.)

Khatchadourian notes that brain implants are unreliable, because they constantly shift in the "gelatinous matter of the cortex." When Scheuermann finally got the robotic arm to bring a chocolate bar to her mouth, she only had time for a nibble before the arm jerked the bar away. Later, the researchers removed Scheuermann's implant because skin was pulling back from the port in her skull, putting her at risk of a "deadly brain infection." [See Note From Reader below.]

Khatchadourian also details how research on brain chips has been militarized. Before Scheuerman's implant was removed, another Darpa contractor, the Applied Physics Laboratory at Johns Hopkins, carried out experiments in which she controlled an F-35 flight simulator with her thoughts.

Thrilled by that demonstration, Darpa ordered more flight-simulation research. Schwartz was reluctant to participate in these experiments, which he saw as stunts with little medical justification. He and Darpa parted ways. Darpa is continuing to fund a program, Mind Flight, in which patients control one or more drones via brain implants.

Khatchadourian raises the possibility that brain chips can be used to control as well as empower implantees. He quotes a *Scientific American* article I wrote about brain-chip pioneer Jose Delgado, who demonstrated more than a half century ago that he could manipulate patients' limbs and emotions via implants. Another researcher, Robert Heath of Tulane, claimed in 1972 that he had used a brain chip to make a gay man sexually responsive to a woman.

I'm skeptical of much of the hype about brain-machine interfaces, and especially memory prostheses, as articles in *Further Reading* indicate. Scientists still know little about how the brain encodes information. Attempts to use brain implants to treat depression and other psychiatric disorders has been disappointing.

Second-rate researchers have conned second-rate Pentagon program managers into believing that science-fiction applications are imminent. That's what I suspect, and hope. But breakthroughs that make bionic solders possible could be around the corner. Cochlear implants, which restore hearing to the deaf via electrodes implanted in auditory nerves, were thought to be impossible until they weren't.

Silicon Valley loves the idea of brain-machine interfaces. Facebook, Google and Elon Musk's firm Neuralink are funding neurotechnology research and hiring former Darpa researchers to do it, according to Gross. Regina Dugan, a former Darpa director who has worked at Facebook and Google, has said that one goal is to allow consumers to type words into a computer simply by thinking, no hands required.

Military officials are already envisioning how neurotechnologies will transform war. That brings me to an essay in *New York Review of Books* by historian Christopher Clark. He reviews *The Future of War: A History*, by military scholar Lawrence Freedman, and *Future War: Preparing for the New Global Battlefield*, by former Air Force Major General Robert Latiff.

The latter "sketches a vision of a future that resembles the fictional scenarios of William Gibson's *Neuromancer*," Clark writes. In future wars a "'metabolically dominant soldier' who enjoys the benefits of immunity to pain, reinforced muscle strength, accelerated healing and 'cognitive enhancement' will enter the battlespace neurally linked not just to his human comrades but also to swarms of semiautonomous bots."

Clark ends his review brooding over the books' implications. "It's hard not to be impressed by the inventiveness of the weapons experts in their underground labs, but hard, too, not to despair at the way in which such ingenuity has been uncoupled from larger ethical imperatives." Clark also deplores the books' assumption that "war is and will always be a human necessity, a feature of our existence as natural as birth or the movement of clouds."

Yes, as my own surveys have shown, most people–scientists, scholars, politicians and soldiers as well as lay folk of all kinds–see war as inevitable and world peace as a pipe dream. I have tried, in vain, to counter this self-fulfilling fatalism in my book *The End of War* and on this blog (again, see below).

Clark ends his review by asking, Where are the "prominent politicians" calling for war's abolition? Good question. Here's another: Where are the prominent scientists calling for war's abolition–or, at the very least, for a moratorium on research that might trigger a terrible new arms race? Let's hope we come to our senses before the era of cyborg warriors begins, because then it might be too late.

Note from Reader:

Dear Mr. Horgan,

Something immediately caught my eye in your article on the Cyborg Soldier; namely that implanted electrodes in the brain are unreliable. From 1967 through 1976, I was employed as a biomedical engineer at the Smith Kettlewell Institute of Visual Sciences at the Pacific Medical Center in San Francisco. My senior investigator was interested in identifying the locus of the dominant Alpha EEG waves as well as other rhythms and was generally investigating so called Visual Evoked Potentials.

The spatial resolution of EEG recording at the time was limited to possibly 16 recording channels at certain defined locations on the scalp. My first assignment was to design and construct a recording instrument with at least 4 times that resolution and the result was a 48 channel EEG recorder which we used in numerous experiments, including some collaboration with Dr.

Derek Fender at the Caltech Biological Information Systems lab, one of my former advisors.

Of course, that system used external skin surface electrodes, as do the systems today which record on the order of 100 simultaneous channels. During that period, another senior investigator at Smith Kettlewell, was interested Brindley's matrix implants over the visual cortex and the resulting phosphene generation. To the point, those electrode arrays and all later ones, designed to interface directly with neural tissue, shift position and degrade in time. Perhaps the most successful long term stimulation implants are the cochlear arrays, which are a rather different animal.

Given also the mechanisms of neural plasticity, yet another variable is added to stimulus and recording electrode interface longevity. Prosthesis to restore to some degree of limb loss or gross nerve trauma are certainly laudable in their intent; one can only hope that the bad dream of the Cyborg Soldier remains a science fiction item. But with advances in genetic engineering and the exploration of non-silicon based electronics, the fascination with the idea in some minds will, I'm afraid, be with us for some time to come.

Julius Madey
Hillsdale, NY

The views expressed are those of the author(s) and are not necessarily those of Scientific American.

About the Author

John Horgan directs the Center for Science Writings at the Stevens Institute of Technology. His books include The End of Science, The End of War *and* Mind-Body Problems, *available for free at mindbodyproblems.com. For many years he wrote the popular blog* Cross Check *for* Scientific American.

Don't Let Robots Pull the Trigger

By The Editors

The killer machines are coming. Robotic weapons that target and destroy without human supervision are poised to start a revolution in warfare comparable to the invention of gunpowder or the atomic bomb. The prospect poses a dire threat to civilians—and could lead to some of the bleakest scenarios in which artificial intelligence runs amok. A prohibition on killer robots, akin to bans on chemical and biological weapons, is badly needed. But some major military powers oppose it.

The robots are no technophobic fantasy. In July 2017, for example, Russia's Kalashnikov Group announced that it had begun development of a camera-equipped 7.62-millimeter machine gun that uses a neural network to make "shoot/no-shoot" decisions. An entire generation of self-controlled armaments, including drones, ships and tanks, is edging toward varying levels of autonomous operation. The U.S. appears to hold a lead in R&D on autonomous systems—with $18 billion slated for investment from 2016 to 2020. But other countries with substantial arms industries are also making their own investments.

Military planners contend that "lethal autonomous weapons systems"—a more anodyne term—could, in theory, bring a detached precision to war fighting. Such automatons could diminish the need for troops and reduce casualties by leaving the machines to battle it out. Yet control by algorithm can potentially morph into "out of control." Existing AI cannot deduce the intentions of others or make critical decisions by generalizing from past experience in the chaos of war. The inability to read behavioral subtleties to distinguish civilian from combatant or friend versus foe should call into question whether AIs should replace GIs in a foreseeable future mission. A killer robot of any kind would be a trained assassin, not unlike Arnold Schwarzenegger in *The Terminator*. After the battle is done, moreover, who would be held responsible when a machine does the killing? The robot? Its owner? Its maker?

With all these drawbacks, a fully autonomous robot fashioned using near-term technology could create a novel threat wielded by smaller nations or terrorists with scant expertise or financial resources. Swarms of tiny, weaponized drones, perhaps even made using 3-D printers, could wreak havoc in densely populated areas. Prototypes are already being tested: the U.S. Department of Defense demonstrated a nonweaponized swarm of more than 100 micro drones in 2016. Stuart Russell of the University of California, Berkeley, a prominent figure in AI research, has suggested that "antipersonnel micro robots" deployed by just a single individual could kill many thousands and constitute a potential weapon of mass destruction.

Since 2013 the United Nations Convention on Certain Conventional Weapons (CCW), which regulates incendiary devices, blinding lasers and other armaments thought to be overly harmful, has debated what to do about lethal autonomous weapons systems. Because of opposition from the U.S., Russia and a few others, the discussions have not advanced to the stage of drafting formal language for a ban. The U.S., for one, has argued that its policy already stipulates that military personnel retain control over autonomous weapons and that premature regulation could put a damper on vital AI research.

A ban need not be overly restrictive. The Campaign to Stop Killer Robots, a coalition of 89 nongovernmental organizations from 50 countries that has pressed for a such a prohibition, emphasizes that it would be limited to offensive weaponry and not extend to antimissile and other defensive systems that automatically fire in response to an incoming warhead.

The current impasse has prompted the campaign to consider rallying at least some nations to agree to a ban outside the forum provided by the CCW, an option used before to kick-start multinational agreements that prohibit land mines and cluster munitions. A preemptive ban on autonomous killing machines, with clear requirements for compliance, would stigmatize the technology and help keep killer robots out of military arsenals.

Since it was first presented at the International Joint Conference on Artificial Intelligence in Stockholm in July, 244 organizations and 3,187 individuals have signed a pledge to "neither participate in nor support the development, manufacture, trade, or use of lethal autonomous weapons." The rationale for making such a pledge was that laws had yet to be passed to bar killer robots. Without such a legal framework, the day may soon come when an algorithm makes the fateful decision to take a human life.

Are Military Bots the Best Way to Clear Improvised Explosive Devices?

By Larry Greenemeier

Hardly a day seems to pass without a new report of a soldier or civilian being killed or maimed by an improvised explosive device (IED) in Afghanistan or Iraq. Just such a weapon killed two coalition members on Monday in Iraq's volatile southern region, according to NATO. Meanwhile, data published October 22 by Wikileaks indicates that IEDs are the biggest killers of British and US troops in Afghanistan, accounting for more than half of all fatalities.

To protect people from these weapons, the U.S. military increasingly relies on robotic bomb detection and disposal units (in addition to the scores of unmanned aerial vehicles (UAVs) overhead with reconnaissance and strike capabilities), creating life-and-death combat relationships between man and machine that will only deepen and proliferate over time.

U.S. and coalition military operating in Afghanistan have experienced about 10,500 roadside bomb incidents so far this year, up from 8,994 in 2009 and 2,677 in 2007, Army Lt. Gen. Michael Oates, director of the Joint Improvised Explosive Device Defeat Organization (JIEDDO), reported October 21. A significant portion of these are IED-related incidents.

The success of such attacks ensures that they will continue for at least the short-term, which means the military is searching for new ways of addressing the problem. In Afghanistan U.S. soldiers conduct month-long Explosive Hazard Reduction courses to train Afghan soldiers about how IEDs work, the threats they pose and techniques for finding them. Coalition forces have spent about $2 billion since 2006 to train soldiers stationed worldwide about IEDs, according to Oates.

A lot of money is also being spent on anti-IED robots. Earlier this month the U.S. Army TACOM Contracting Center in Warren, Mich., ordered $14 million worth of robot intelligence software and spare parts for its PackBot tactical mobile robots, made by iRobot in Bedford, Mass. This was TACOM's 20th such order for iRobot technology and part of the unit's larger $286-million "xBot" contract for purchasing bomb-detection robots.

There are more than 3,500 iRobot devices serving in the U.S. military as well as the armed forces of another 20 allied countries, says Joseph Dyer, iRobot's chief operating officer and a retired U.S. Navy vice admiral. *Scientific American* spoke with Dyer about the role that robots are playing in modern warfare and where the technology is headed.

[An edited transcript of the interview follows.]

Q: The military's reluctance to rely on robots in combat situations has changed dramatically in recent years. Why is that?

A: Interest in robotic devices really started with unmanned aerial vehicles in the early 1980s and the RQ-2 Pioneer UAV [developed by AAI, which is now part of Textron Systems Corp., and Israel Aerospace Industries]. The change necessary to adopt, much less embrace, unmanned aircraft first encountered resistance from the white-scarf system of fighter pilots who believed that an unmanned system couldn't do the things a human pilot could do. While there's still some resistance to unmanned vehicles, the realities of war are changing that. Whereas there was a standoffish attitude with the white scarves regarding robotic vehicles in the air, with the Army the soldiers realized robots could do the things the soldiers themselves really didn't want to do. The Army's mission is up close and personal, dangerous and dirty. Consider this: it took 20 years for the unmanned aircraft market to become a half-billion-dollar industry, but it took the newer market for unmanned ground systems only half as long to reach a half-billion dollars.

Q: What is it about the combat in Iraq and Afghanistan that has created a demand for land-based robotic devices?

A: In urban and desert terrains robots contribute anywhere you need distance between your body and bad things happening. Urban warfare, even for an Army and Marine Corps as accomplished as ours, is scary stuff and fraught with issues of collateral damage and risk to noncombatants.

Q: How are robots typically used in combat situations today?

A: Of the 3,500 iRobot devices serving the military, the majority of them are helping with explosive ordinance disposal (EOD). Normally, troops will be told about an explosive device or actually find an IED. These soldiers will then call in the threat to specialists who investigate and possibly engage the IED with the aid of a robot, which can be used to send video of the device to an EOD team standing out of the device's range and/or to dispose of the device. In both Iraq and Afghanistan, because of the proliferation of IEDs and the fact that you don't have enough EOD troops to be everywhere they're needed, there's also a strong desire for non-EOD teams to use robots for what's known as route clearance, where the robots will help identify and possibly clear roadside IEDs. During the next phase of use, robots will not just be focused on IEDs or road clearance but rather on becoming a real player in the infantry.

Q: A player in what sense? How is the military's use of robots changing?

A: Let me tell you a story. In a battlefield exercise about three years ago at Fort Benning, Georgia, one where many new technologies including robots and new UAVs and wearable computers and all of those things were being tested in a war game, an Army captain leading one of the teams was asked which of these technologies he would want to take with him to combat today. He said he would take iRobot's small unmanned ground vehicle (SUGV) [used for surveillance, reconnaissance and/or bomb disposal] and AeroVironment's Raven UAV. The captain explained, "I want situational awareness on the battlefield, and I want it from God's view, and I want it from up close and personal. If I have foreknowledge of the battlefield, it ensures the survivability of my troops and the success of my mission."

The next phase of this, which is just beginning, is robot autonomy. This is probably less exciting than most people would believe. Whereas today you have a soldier using a joystick to manipulate a robot much like a video game, what's next are a few pieces of autonomy that enable the robot to take over some of its own navigation, like cruise control. I don't have to drive the robot every step of the way, I can tell it to maintain a certain vector while traveling. Another area of autonomy is to program robots to, when they lose their communication signal with the troops, automatically navigate back to the last position where it could send and receive a signal. Today, if a robot loses communication, you have to go out and get it, which is not a popular thing. If you wanted to be out there in the field, you wouldn't have sent a robot in the first place. Little by little, robots will be able to autonomously complete more and more complex assignments to the point where you can program them with actual missions.

Q: What types of robotic missions are we talking about?

A: Today, the ratio of robots to operators is one to one. You're going to start to have one operator with multiple robots that can be operated in a swarm, carrying out coordinated tasks. For an example of how this might work go back to the 9/11 time frame when we had anthrax in the Capitol Building offices. We couldn't even get in there for days. Now you have robots that could go in there and do chemical and biological testing and even create maps that would give you an understanding of the dangers and where they are located within the building.

Q: How are robots themselves changing to meet the demands of ground combat?

A: If you go back and look at the early days of airplanes and even hot-air balloons, they began as tactical reconnaissance technologies. Then, once you got frustrated at being able to see the action but not do anything about it, the technology was given new features such as the ability to fire weapons. Robots likewise started out this way. We're not there in terms of giving robots strike capabilities yet, but in time we will see armed robots.

Q: Would armed robots pose a danger to both sides in a combat situation, especially if there is a malfunction?

A: In terms of lethality it's our position that you're always going to have a man in the loop, even if a lot of the press and all of Hollywood don't see it that way. Will we have autonomous lethal systems? I don't think so. I don't think it's ethically right, and I don't foresee a world that hands over life-and-death decisions to a machine, even if it's a very capable system.

About the Author

Larry Greenemeier is the associate editor of technology for Scientific American, *covering a variety of tech-related topics, including biotech, computers, military tech, nanotech and robots.*

To Clear Deadly Land Mines, Science Turns to Drones and Machine Learning

By Andrew Robinson and Dominic Smith

A warm wind blows across an empty field on the outskirts of Pawnee, Okla. A small group of researchers struggle against the stiff wind to set up a pop-up tent for some shade. Nearby a young man opens a heavy Pelican case to reveal a pile of explosives. "These are inert," he says, "but we're lucky to be working at a range that has so many different kinds of munitions."

The range is an explosive-ordnance-disposal field laboratory maintained by Oklahoma State University, and the researchers are led by Jasper Baur and Gabriel Steinberg, co-founders of the Demining Research Community, a nonprofit organization bridging academic research and humanitarian demining efforts. They have been in Oklahoma for two weeks, setting up grids of mines and munitions to train a drone-based, machine-learning-powered detection system to find and identify dangerous explosives so humans don't have to.

The Landmine and Cluster Munition Monitor reports that at least 7,073 people were killed or injured by mines in 54 countries and areas in 2020. Many of the groups working to remove these old munitions are nonprofits with a fraction of the resources of the militaries that deployed the dangerous explosives.

Steinberg holds up a small plastic wing attached to a metal piece shaped like a spark plug. "This is the PFM-1 'butterfly mine,'" he says. This antipersonnel mine was developed by the Soviet Union and deployed in its war in Afghanistan, where examples of the munition can be found to this day. There is evidence the same mines are currently being deployed by Russia in Ukraine.

The primary goal of mines and unexploded cluster munitions is to deny the use of roads and fields to enemy troops and vehicles. The problem is that mines and unexploded cluster munitions don't "turn off" when a war ends. Instead they remain as a deadly hazard to civilians for decades, sometimes outlasting the very countries who deployed them.

There are many millions of active mines and munitions estimated to be scattered in dozens of countries. Baur says his and his colleagues' goal is to make their drone-detection system available to demining organizations around the world to aid in efforts to make post conflict countries safe.

With countries continuing to deploy munitions in the war in Ukraine and elsewhere, the need for new tools will persist for some time.

About the Authors

Andrew Robinson is a documentary producer, journalist, and writer living in Los Angeles, CA. His Emmy Award–winning production company, Smith Robinson Multimedia produces long and short form video focusing on science and the outdoors.

Dominic Smith is an Emmy winning multimedia producer, visual effects artist and journalist based in New Hampshire. He operates Smith Robinson Multimedia with offices in New England and California.

AI-Influenced Weapons Need Better Regulation

By Branka Marijan

With Russia's invasion of Ukraine as the backdrop, the United Nations recently held a meeting to discuss the use of autonomous weapons systems, commonly referred to as killer robots. These are essentially weapons that are programmed to find a class of targets, then select and attack a specific person or object within that class, with little human control over the decisions that are made.

Russia took center stage in this discussion, in part because of its potential capabilities in this space, but also because its diplomats thwarted the effort to discuss these weapons, saying sanctions made it impossible to properly participate. For a discussion that to date had been far too slow, Russia's spoiling slowed it down even further.

I have been tracking the development of autonomous weapons and attending the UN discussions on the issue for over seven years, and Russia's aggression is becoming an unfortunate test case for how artificial intelligence (AI)–fueled warfare can and likely will proceed.

The technology behind some of these weapons systems is immature and error-prone, and there is little clarity on how the systems function and make decisions. Some of these weapons will invariably hit the wrong targets, and competitive pressures might result in deployment of more systems that are not ready for the battelfield.

To avoid the loss of innocent lives and the destruction of critical infrastructure in Ukraine and beyond, we need nothing less that the strongest diplomatic effort to prohibit in some cases, and regulate, in others, the use of these weapons and the technologies behind them, including AI and machine learning. This is critical because when military operations are proceeding poorly countries might be tempted to use new technologies to gain an advantage. An example of this is Russia's KUB-BLA loitering munition, which has the ability to identify targets using AI.

Data fed into AI-based systems can teach remote weapons what a target looks like, and what to do upon reaching that target. While similar to facial recognition tools, AI technologies for military use have different implications, particularly when they are meant to destroy and kill, and as such, experts have raised concerns about their introduction into dynamic war contexts. And while Russia may have been successful in thwarting real-time discussion of these weapons, it isn't alone. The U.S., India and Israel are all fighting regulation of these dangerous systems.

AI might be more mature and well-known in its use in cyberwarfare, including to supercharge malware attacks or to better impersonate trusted users in order to access to critical infrastructure, such as the electric grid. But, major powers are using it to develop physically destructive weapons. Russia has already made important advances in autonomous tanks, machines that can run without human operators who could theoretically override mistakes, while the United States has demonstrated a number of capabilities, including munitions that can destroy a surface vessel using a swarm of drones. AI is employed in the development of swarming technologies and loitering munitions, also called kamikaze drones. Rather than the futuristic robots seen in science-fiction movies, these systems use previously existing military platforms that leverage AI technologies. Simply, a few lines of code and new sensors can make a difference in whether a military system is functioning autonomously or under human control. Crucially, introducing AI into decision-making by militaries could lead to overrealiance on the technology, shaping military decision-making and potentially escalating conflicts.

AI-based warfare might seem like a video game, but last September, according to Secretary of the Air Force Frank Kendall, the U.S. Air Force, for the first time, used AI to help to identify a target or targets in "a live operational kill chain." Presumably, this means AI was used to identify and kill human targets.

Little information was provided about the mission, including whether any casualties that occurred were the intended targets. What inputs were used to identify such individuals and could there have been possible errors in identification? AI technologies have been shown to be biased, particularly against women and people in minority communities. False identifications disproportionately impact already marginalized and racialized groups.

If recent social media discussions among the AI community are any indication, the developers, largely from the private sector, who are creating the new technologies that some militaries are already deploying are largely unaware of their impact. Tech journalist Jeremy Kahn argues in *Fortune* that a dangerous disconnect exists between developers and leading militaries, including U.S. and Russian, which are using AI in decision-making and data analysis. The developers seem to be unaware of the general-purpose nature of some of the tools they are building and how militaries could use them in warfare, including to target civilians.

Undoubtedly, lessons from the current invasion will also shape the technology projects the militaries pursue. At the moment, the United States is at the head of the pack, but a joint statement by Russia and China in early February notes that they aim to "jointly build international relations of a new type," and specifically points to their aim to shape governance of new technologies, including what I believe will be military uses of AI.

Independently, the U.S. and its allies are developing norms on responsible military uses of AI, but generally are not talking with potential adversaries. In general, states with more technologically advanced militaries have been unwilling to accept any constraints on the developments of AI technology. This is where international diplomacy is critical: there must be constraints on these types of weapons, and everyone has to agree to shared standards and transparency in use of the technologies.

The war in Ukraine should be a wake-up call regarding the use of technology in warfare, and the need to regulate AI technologies to ensure civilian protection. Unchecked and potentially hasty development of military applications of artificial intelligence will continue to undermine international humanitarian law and norms regarding civilian protection. Though the international order is in disarray, the solutions to current and future crises are diplomatic, not military, and the next gathering of the U.N. or another group needs to rapidly address this new era of warfare.

About the Author

Branka Marijan is a senior researcher at Project Ploughshares, where she leads research on the military and security implications of emerging technologies. She is a contributor to the Center for International Governance Innovation.

Section 3: It Came from the Lab

Shocking Pink: An Inexpensive Test for Chemical Weapon Attacks

By Larry Greenemeier

It seems unlikely that the maker of hundred-million-dollar Hollywood blockbusters such as *Armageddon* and *The Transformers* could inspire scientists to develop an ultralow-cost tool for quickly sensing airborne chemical weapons. Yet one former University of Michigan at Ann Arbor (U.M.) researcher says his idea to use a nerve-gas antidote to create an inexpensive litmus paper–like nerve-gas sensor emerged shortly after watching *The Rock* on DVD a few years ago.

During the climax of that 1996 Michael Bay movie, chemical weapons specialist Stanley Goodspeed (played by Nicholas Cage) injects himself in the heart with atropine to prevent certain death from VX gas. After watching the movie with his wife, Jiseok Lee became intrigued by the possibility of using the nerve-agent antidote pralidoxime (also known as 2-PAM) to detect the presence of organophosphate nerve gases such as VX and sarin.

"I was inspired to use an antidote because an antidote always has a nice affinity to poison," says Lee, now a postdoctoral associate in the Massachusetts Institute of Technology's Department of Chemical Engineering. "That was the start of this research."

Lee and his U.M. colleagues were able to detect the presence of a nerve agent related to sarin gas at a low concentration of 160 parts per billion using a litmus-like paper sensor designed to change color from blue to pink (Lee says although it looks pink, technically, it is red) within 30 seconds of exposure to trace amounts of the toxic gas. The sensor combines a group of atoms from a nerve gas antidote with a molecule that changes color when it is under stress, the researchers reported recently in the online version of *Advanced Functional Materials*.

"The test can be done using a simple filter paper, and the sensory materials can be synthesized quite easily," says Jinsang Kim, an associate professor in U.M.'s Materials Science and Engineering; Chemical Engineering; and Biomedical Engineering departments. Kim, who advised Lee and his colleagues during their research, adds that it costs about $1 for the chemical reagents and solvents used to make each filter.

"This work is very novel in that we don't need complicated lab-scale analytical devices," Lee says. "[With some] technical modification we might be able to easily commercialize the sensor with extremely low cost."

A litmus-paper test is a low-tech alternative to some of the more sophisticated chemical and radiation detection tools developed in recent years. These include self-contained mobile land and airborne laboratories for monitoring air quality, which the U.S. Environmental Protection Agency (EPA) has poured millions of dollars into over the past decade. The EPA's Trace Atmospheric Gas Analyzer (TAGA) bus performs real-time sampling and analysis to detect chemicals at very low levels; and the agency's Airborne Spectral Photometric Environmental Collection Technology (ASPECT) aircraft uses chemical and radiological detectors, high-resolution digital photography, video and GPS technology combined with sophisticated software to remotely detect chemicals and radiation. In addition, handheld Chemical Agent Monitor (CAM) devices used by the military and first responders weigh several kilograms and cost upward of $6,500. CAM devices, of course, are also more sophisticated than litmus paper, detecting and discriminating between, for example, vapors of nerve and blister agents and displaying their relative concentration.

Paper-based sensors would be a more practical alternative in equipping large numbers of soldiers and first responders. Litmus paper could warn them to don gas masks, even if specific details about a particular chemical attack aren't available.

The Michigan researchers are now developing a way for sensory chemicals to self-assemble into nanofibers that could be used to make a new type of sensor device that provides three different sensory signals–color change, fluorescence development and conductivity change–that can alert to the presence of a number of chemical and even biological weapons such as anthrax, Kim says.

Perhaps the biggest litmus test lies ahead–finding a way to commercialization these technologies and put them in the hands of those who need them the most.

About the Author

Larry Greenemeier is the associate editor of technology for Scientific American, *covering a variety of tech-related topics, including biotech, computers, military tech, nanotech and robots.*

How Can Minute Quantities of Chemicals Such as Sarin Overwhelm the Nervous System of an Adult Human So Quickly?

By Michael Allswede

The four factors that determine how a chemical will affect the human body are absorption, distribution, elimination and potency. Absorption refers to the ability of the chemical to enter the body rapidly. In newsworthy events involving carfentanyl and sarin, victims were dosed by way of vapor exposure. In these instances absorption occurred through the lungs, which have a huge surface area and are very efficient at taking up chemicals. Nicotine blood levels in a smoker, for example, rise almost immediately after inhalation. In contrast, absorption through the skin or clothing requires a greater dose and more time and may not occur at all if the chemical cannot penetrate the skin, as in the case of carfentanyl.

Distribution refers to where in the body the chemical goes to exert its effects. To infiltrate the nervous system, a chemical must possess a certain degree of lipid (fat) solubility. Carfentanyl and sarin both rapidly penetrate the lipid brain barrier. Elimination describes how fast the body can rid itself of the chemical and recover from its effects.

A chemicals potency is its ability to exert effects at its site of action. The most potent chemicals act on physiologic receptors within the body and the degree of binding of the chemical to the receptor determines its potency. Carfentanyl binds to the human opiate receptor thousands of times stronger than morphine or heroin does. Indeed, the fentanyl family of synthetic opiates was developed as rapid-acting, high-potency anesthesia medication: carfentanyl overdose causes death by rapidly sedating the individual and halting breathing.

Sarin's potency stems from the inhibition of a very important enzyme in the body called acetyl cholinesterase. This enzyme acts as an off switch to the part of the nervous system that controls voluntary movements such as breathing, as well as bronchial constriction secretion, urinary and bowel continence, and other involuntary functions. When acetyl cholinesterase is inhibited, the nervous system is over-stimulated and the body is paralyzed, breathing stops and the lungs no longer function. Because there is only a small amount of acetyl cholinesterase in the body, very little sarin is needed to induce this effect.

The combination of rapid absorption through the lungs, rapid distribution to the sites of activity, and high potency produces the swiftly lethal toxic effect observed in both carfentanyl and sarin vapor exposure. Vapor toxicity is described in terms of the lethal concentration-time product, or LCt50. LCt50 refers to the death of 50 percent of subjects exposed to a certain concentration over a certain time. For example, the LCt50 for isopropyl methylhosphonofluridate, or sarin, is 100 milligrams per minute per cubic meter. (100 milligrams of pure sarin would look like a small droplet.) That means that if a person is breathing air with a concentration of 100 milligrams per cubic meter, she will live about one minute before she has a 50 percent chance of dying. Smaller people or those breathing faster will be the most susceptible in the event of exposure.

About the Author

Michael Allswede is an emergency physician and medical toxicologist at the University of Pittsburgh and a senior research fellow at the University's Center for Biosecurity. He is the author of the RaPiD-T Program (Recognition, Protection, Decontamination, and Treatment) and has trained first responders in chemical weapon management since 1997.

Fake Botox, Real Threat

By Ken Coleman and Raymond A. Zilinskas

In early 2006 a self-styled "naturopathic" doctor, Chad Livdahl, pleaded guilty in Arizona to mail fraud and conspiracy to engage in mail and wire fraud, to misbrand a drug and to defraud the U.S. He was sentenced to nine years in prison. His wife and business partner in Toxin Research International, Inc., in Tucson, Zarah Karim, pleaded guilty to the same charges and received a six-year sentence. Both also paid heavy fines and restitution because, according to prosecutors, the couple had made at least $1.5 million in just more than a year by peddling tiny vials of fake Botox to doctors across the U.S.

Botox, which is injected in minute amounts to smooth frown lines or relax muscle spasms, is far from the only medical product that inspires illicit manufacture and trade. The world market in counterfeit pharmaceuticals is estimated to be worth some $75 billion annually. But the active ingredient in Botox and related products differs from the constituents of other pharmaceuticals in a profound way: in its pure form, it is the deadliest substance known to science. In fact, botulinum neurotoxin (BoNT) is grouped with the world's most lethal potential biological weapons agents, sharing "Select Agent" status with the pathogens that cause smallpox, anthrax and plague. This biowarfare potential puts the existence of illicit laboratories churning out the toxin and of shady distributors selling it worldwide through the Internet into a more disturbing light than most pharmaceutical fraud.

As security analysts, we undertook two years ago to explore the size and nature of this illicit global trade and have come away gravely concerned that a deadly, but once relatively inaccessible, weapons agent is now becoming as easy to get or to make as a roadside bomb. We also believe concrete steps that are inexpensive and without risk could begin to reduce this threat and should be taken as soon as possible.

A Multitiered Market

Since 1989, when the U.S. Food and Drug Administration licensed Allergan in Irvine, Calif., to sell Botox for medical uses, the company has garnered the major share of the legitimate market for botulinum toxin products, worth some $2 billion in sales in 2009. Other manufacturers of licensed BoNT products, particularly Ipsen, based in France, Merz Pharma in Germany and Lanzhou Institute of Biological Products in China, are making inroads, however, and in some countries outselling Allergan. The FDA approved cosmetic applications of BoNT in 2002, and today a total of only seven companies in the world have licenses to produce pharmaceutical-grade botulinum toxin for use in people. Many other companies, three of them in the U.S., supply laboratories with so-called reagent-grade BoNT, which is not approved for human use but rather for industrial and scientific applications, such as vaccine research.

Counterfeit products are sometimes mislabeled to resemble an authentic pharmaceutical brand or more often are given a sound-alike name, such as "Butox" or "Beauteous." Some are fakes in every sense, lacking any detectable BoNT, but one study published last year by Ipsen investigators Andy Pickett and Martin Mewies found that about 80 percent of the illicit BoNT products they tested did contain some of the toxin, albeit in widely varying amounts. The primary customers for these bootleg BoNT products, which typically sell for less than the legitimate versions, are unscrupulous doctors and cosmetologists who buy from illicit producers or middlemen, often via the Internet, hoping to pocket the price difference. Makers of genuine BoNT products estimate that this counterfeit market costs them hundreds of millions of dollars a year in lost sales.

The cost to people who receive counterfeit products is potentially much higher, as a 2004 incident in Florida illustrates. Vials of counterfeit cosmetic BoNT landed four people in the hospital for months, near death with severe botulism and in need of mechanical ventilation. A doctor with a suspended license had purchased the BoNT from a licensed reagent-grade producer, then injected three patients and himself with a massive overdose of toxin. Exactly how much toxin each person received is unclear, but the doctor had made the grave mistake of confusing units (one unit is equivalent to 4.8 nanograms of BoNT, or 4.8 billionths of a gram) with micrograms (μg), or millionths of a gram.*

Other cases of reagent-grade material illegally resold for human use have also been documented, and some evidence suggests that legitimate pharmaceutical-grade product has on rare occasion been stolen or diverted to the black market. The great majority of counterfeit products, however, have mysterious origins, mainly in Asia, and are offered by illicit sellers who may or may not also be making their own ingredients.

In China alone we found 20 entities–they represent themselves as companies–that claim on their Web sites to be "certified" suppliers of BoNT and to offer cosmetic products for sale. The addresses provided on the sites often proved to be nonexistent locations or small offices that appeared to be empty fronts. Whatever the real nature of the entities behind these Web sites, they have access to genuine botulinum toxin, as the Ipsen analyses demonstrated.

Evidence suggests that the manufacture of counterfeit BoNT products has also spread to the former Soviet Union and that criminal gangs may be involved. Counterfeit pharmaceuticals have been a common problem in Russia for some time, so we were not surprised to learn from experts there that an estimated 90 percent of Russian cosmetology clinics are using counterfeit BoNT products at least some of the time. One security consultant described a purveyor of counterfeit BoNT products that has been operating in Russia for more than three years. The source of these products is reportedly located somewhere in Chechnya, and its representative flies regularly to St. Petersburg carrying suitcases filled with vials bearing labels almost identical to legitimate Botox packaging. When one client asked how much product could be purchased, the representative is alleged to have replied that any quantity, even 1,000 vials, could be supplied.

We believe there is a danger that India's counterfeit drug producers, if not already involved in the illicit BoNT business, soon will be as well. The country has a legitimate producer of a BoNT product called BOTOGenie, launched in 2007, and a vibrant domestic market for both cosmetic and therapeutic BoNT products. The Indian medical tourism industry catering to foreigners seeking inexpensive care is also expanding rapidly, which is likely to entice the country's well-documented pharmaceutical counterfeiting rings to cash in.

From a security perspective, this booming market is troubling because, for manufacturer-distributors it is only a small step from selling counterfeit BoNT products for cosmetic uses to selling the botulinum toxin itself in bulk quantities directly to subversive interests. Indeed, as the Russian example illustrates, such distinctions may already be blurred. And there is little to stop counterfeiters or criminals from setting up a manufacturing facility, because making botulinum toxin requires no exotic equipment and only moderate expertise in microbiology.

Easy to Make, Harder to Deploy

Clostridium botulinum, the bacterium that produces BoNT, exists naturally in soil, but it is anaerobic, meaning that it thrives only in oxygen-free conditions. In the past, the most common source of botulinum toxin poisoning–botulism–in the U.S. was food, such as damaged or unsterilized canned goods. The more common form in adults today is wound botulism, which occurs mostly among addicts who infect themselves with *C. botulinum* while injecting drugs.

The pure toxin that the microbes generate is, on its own, the most potent poison in the world. And manufacturing the minuscule amounts of it that are required to kill takes only equipment standard in biology laboratories worldwide. In less than a month, someone with the equivalent of a master's degree in biology could probably accomplish the necessary steps to produce enough toxin to cause mass casualties.

BoNT is so potent that a single *molecule* of toxin is believed to be capable of incapacitating one nerve cell. The toxin particles block receptors on nerve endings, silencing the nerves and paralyzing surrounding muscles. When pure BoNT is injected into a vein or muscle, just 0.09 to 0.15 μg can kill a 70-kilogram person. Although inhalation delivers the toxin to nerve fibers less efficiently, a mere 0.70 to 0.90 μg of inhaled toxin can be deadly to an adult. Ingesting BoNT is actually the least effective method of poisoning oneself, requiring 70 μg. Put another way, one gram of BoNT potentially contains more than 14,000 lethal doses delivered orally or about 1.25 million lethal doses if inhaled.

All *C. botulinum* strains found in nature are capable of producing BoNT, although the strains used by legitimate manufacturers are naturally occurring hyperproducers of toxin. One in particular, known as the Hall strain, is also widely employed in academic labs and stored in national cell culture collections. A would-be toxin manufacturer with access to the bacterium would have no problem finding out how to use it because instructions have been widely published in the scientific literature over the past 50 years.

The process begins with a small colony of *C. botulinum*, suspended in a common nutrient broth and allowed to multiply in incubators and fermenters for a total of three to four days. This mixture is then removed from the fermenter and centrifuged or filtered to separate out the liquid containing concentrated toxin. Of course, the pharmaceutical industry performs additional purification steps to ensure the quality and stability of their final product, which is sold as a fine powder packaged in a small vial. When the end user is ready to reconstitute the material, adding 10 milliliters of saline to the vial dissolves the powder in seconds. This liquid formulation must then be used within a few hours, because it quickly loses potency.

The relative fragility of the toxin once it is exposed to the environment has been a substantial obstacle in past efforts to weaponize BoNT. The U.S. and U.S.S.R. nonetheless succeeded in developing weapons that dispersed BoNT as an aerosol. Iraq developed BoNT-containing bombs, which would probably have been next to useless. The only well-documented attempt by a nonstate actor to deploy botulinum toxin as a weapon occurred in the early 1990s. The apocalyptic Japanese cult Aum Shinrikyo, whose membership included medical doctors and a scientist, attempted several times to disperse aerosolized BoNT through sprayers hidden in briefcases. These attacks failed, but only because the strain of *C. botulinum* the group's scientist used was a poor toxin producer, sprayer nozzles got clogged and some guilt-ridden operatives failed to activate their devices.

The most plausible scenarios for terrorist use of BoNT involve sabotage of food or beverages. One study published in the *Proceedings of the National Academy of Sciences USA* in 2005 analyzed possible strategies for introducing the toxin at key points in the cow-to-consumer milk supply chain. The paper provoked controversy for identifying a sabotage method that might succeed. Yet its authors, Lawrence M. Wein and Yifan Liu of Stanford University, could not have known five years ago that terrorists attempting this kind of attack today would be able to purchase the toxin needed for their plan from an anonymous Internet source instead of having to manufacture it themselves. Their hypothetical plot now seems that much easier to carry out.

Assessing the Threat

Attempts by the international security community to prevent the proliferation of biological and chemical weapons usually focus on limiting demand by pressuring countries not to engage in weapons development and constraining supply by tightly controlling traffic in weapons-making equipment and know-how. Export controls and treaties, such as the 1972 Biological and Toxin Weapons Convention and the 1993 Chemical Weapons Convention, were developed by governments for governments, however. The international proliferation of illicit botulinum toxin products creates an entirely new and perplexing situation because the toxin-making supplies are not sought by governments but by individuals and because demand for the toxin is not driven by governments but by consumers.

The unique and important role of the Internet in both facilitating supply and in driving demand also makes the proliferation of the botulinum toxin threat more immediate than is the case for any other potential biological or chemical weapon. Our study documented a substantial increase in Internet vendors in the past two years, yet the possibility that these sellers represent a comparable proliferation in illicit BoNT manufacturers has not yet garnered much attention from agencies charged with preventing bioterrorism or suppressing the counterfeit pharmaceutical trade. Instead it is falling into the cracks between the two jurisdictions.

Indeed, some traditional weapons-interdiction strategies are likely to be ineffective against this novel threat. Attempting to affect the supply side of this equation by limiting equipment or information, for example, cannot seriously deter would-be BoNT manufacturers because the commonplace materials needed to make the toxin and the bacterium itself are too widespread.

Limiting demand for counterfeits might help discourage illicit manufacturers. Producers of pharmaceutical-grade toxin are employing advanced labeling technologies, such as holograms and verifiable serial numbers on packages so that doctors and cosmetologists can be assured they have genuine products. To educate end users about the dangers of counterfeits, Ipsen researchers have also made parts of their analyses of counterfeit products available to the public in lectures, poster sessions and scientific articles.

Allergan has taken quiet and selective steps toward stemming counterfeiting, including collaborating with investigators in China to close down one illicit BoNT operation in Shanxi Province. Because the number of illegal BoNT laboratories is large and likely to increase, however, companies have neither the expertise, the resources nor the authority needed to track down and prosecute these criminals.

A different example of pharmaceutical counterfeiting may offer a more effective approach. Only a few years ago the antimalaria drug artesunate had become the object of a robust counterfeit market. By 2007 one third to one half of all artesunate sold in Southeast Asia was actually counterfeit product, most of it therapeutically useless. As a result, licensed artesunate manufacturers were not only losing money, malaria victims were dying and the disease was spreading because so many patients were going untreated. That same year, a relatively complex international cooperative effort code-named Operation Jupiter was mounted for the specific purpose of suppressing this counterfeit artesunate trade. Collaborators in the offensive included representatives from the Wellcome Trust, Interpol, the Royal Canadian Mounted Police, the Australian Therapeutic Goods Administration, the Intellectual Property Division of the Chinese Ministry of Public Security, the World Health Organization, the U.S. Centers for Disease Control and Prevention, and several other smaller agencies and nongovernmental organizations.

Although Operation Jupiter holds many lessons for attempts to suppress counterfeit drugs, one of the project's most notable and important activities was the collection of hundreds of samples of counterfeit artesunate sold at five different sites in Cambodia, Laos, Myanmar (Burma), Thailand and Vietnam. These samples were transported to high-quality reference laboratories and subjected to detailed analyses that constructed a "product signature" for each sample. These unique profiles allowed analysts to deduce how many different illicit artesunate producers were operating, and with that information in hand, law-enforcement agents could begin matching the products sold by intermediaries to the original manufacturers and sketching the outlines of distribution networks. In this way, at least some of the counterfeit products were traced to southeast China, enabling officials there to break up that criminal operation.

We do not delude ourselves about how difficult it would be to convince governments to partake in such an effort against counterfeit botulinum toxin producers. We do believe the Operation Jupiter example is relevant because it offers a scientific approach to at least beginning to understand the scope of the problem. If law-enforcement agencies took just the first step of setting up phony clinics to buy illicit BoNT products, then laboratory analyses could begin to establish how many illegal producers are operating. The data could later be used to pursue the criminals or could point to possible toxin sources in the event of an attack.

As security analysts, we know there are myriad theoretical threats to public safety. Only very few biological and chemical agents can be used by nonstate actors to cause mass casualties, however, and now none is as easy to procure as BoNT, because of illicit manufacturing and Internet trade. Vanity is currently driving the highly profitable market for counterfeit BoNT products, but it would be folly to assume that subversives have not noticed that booming business, too.

**Erratum (8/13/10): The correct conversion is 100 units equals 4.8 nanograms.*

About the Authors

Ken Coleman and Raymond A. Zilinskas collaborate at the James Martin Center for Nonproliferation Studies of the Monterey Institute of International Studies in California. Coleman, a former microbiologist, is a senior fellow at the institute and a medical technology entrepreneur. Zilinskas, also a former microbiologist, directs the center's chemical and biological weapons nonproliferation program. He has been a longtime consultant to the U.S. government and was a United Nations inspector in Iraq in 1994.

AI Drug Discovery Systems Might Be Repurposed to Make Chemical Weapons, Researchers Warn

By Rebecca Sohn

In 2020 Collaborations Pharmaceuticals, a company that specializes in looking for new drug candidates for rare and communicable diseases, received an unusual request. The private Raleigh, N.C., firm was asked to make a presentation at an international conference on chemical and biological weapons. The talk dealt with how artificial intelligence software, typically used to develop drugs for treating, say, Pitt-Hopkins syndrome or Chagas disease, might be sidetracked for more nefarious purposes.

In responding to the invitation, Sean Ekins, Collaborations' chief executive, began to brainstorm with Fabio Urbina, a senior scientist at the company. It did not take long for them to come up with an idea: What if, instead of using animal toxicology data to avoid dangerous side effects for a drug, Collaborations put its AI-based MegaSyn software to work generating a compendium of toxic molecules that were similar to VX, a notorious nerve agent?

The team ran MegaSyn overnight and came up with 40,000 substances, including not only VX but other known chemical weapons, as well as many completely new potentially toxic substances. All it took was a bit of programming, open-source data, a 2015 Mac computer and less than six hours of machine time. "It just felt a little surreal," Urbina says, remarking on how the software's output was similar to the company's commercial drug-development process. "It wasn't any different from something we had done before–use these generative models to generate hopeful new drugs."

Collaborations presented the work at Spiez CONVERGENCE, a conference in Switzerland that is held every two years to assess new trends in biological and chemical research that might pose threats to national security. Urbina, Ekins and their colleagues even published a peer-reviewed commentary on the company's research in the journal *Nature Machine Intelligence*—and went on to give a briefing on the findings to the White House Office of Science and Technology Policy. "Our sense is that [the research] could form a useful springboard for policy development in this area," says Filippa Lentzos, co-director of the Center for Science and Security Studies at King's College London and a co-author of the paper.

The eerie resemblance to the company's day-to-day routine work was startling. The researchers had previously used MegaSyn to generate molecules with therapeutic potential that have the same molecular target as VX, Urbina says. These drugs, called acetylcholinesterase inhibitors, can help treat neurodegenerative conditions such as Alzheimer's. For their study, the researchers had merely asked the software to generate substances similar to VX without inputting the exact structure of the molecule.

Many drug discovery AIs, including MegaSyn, use artificial neural networks. "Basically, the neural net is telling us which roads to take to lead to a specific destination, which is the biological activity," says Alex MacKerell, director of the Computer-Aided Drug Design Center at the University of Maryland School of Pharmacy, who was not involved in the research. The AI systems "score" a molecule based on certain criteria, such as how well it either inhibits or activates a specific protein. A higher score tells researchers that the substance might be more likely to have the desired effect.

In its study, the company's scoring method revealed that many of the novel molecules MegaSyn generated were predicted to be more toxic than VX, a realization that made both Urbina and Ekins uncomfortable. They wondered if they had already crossed an ethical boundary by even running the program and decided not to do anything further to computationally narrow down the results, much less test the substances in any way.

"I think their ethical intuition was exactly right," says Paul Root Wolpe, a bioethicist and director of the Center for Ethics at Emory University, who was not involved in the research. Wolpe frequently writes and thinks about issues related to emerging technologies such as artificial intelligence. Once the authors felt they could demonstrate that this was a potential threat, he says, "their obligation was not to push it any further."

But some experts say that the research did not suffice to answer important questions about whether using AI software to find toxins could practically lead to the development of an actual biological weapon.

"The development of actual weapons in past weapons programs have shown, time and again, that what seems possible theoretically may not be possible in practice," comments Sonia Ben Ouagrham-Gormley, an associate professor at the Schar School of Policy and Government's biodefense program at George Mason University, who was not involved with the research.

Despite that challenge, the ease with which an AI can rapidly generate a vast quantity of potentially hazardous substances could still speed up the process of creating lethal bioweapons, says Elana Fertig, associate director of quantitative sciences at the Sidney Kimmel Comprehensive Cancer Center at Johns Hopkins University, who was also not involved in the research.

To make it harder for people to misuse these technologies, the authors of the paper propose several ways to monitor and control who can use these technologies and how they are used, including wait lists that would require users to undergo a prescreening process to verify their credentials before they could access models, data or code that could be readily misused.

They also suggest presenting drug discovery AIs to the public through an application programming interface (API), which is an intermediary that lets two pieces of software talk to each other. A user would have to specifically request molecule data from the API. In an e-mail to *Scientific American*, Ekins wrote that an API could be structured to only generate molecules that would minimize potential toxicity and "demand the users [apply] the tools/models in a specific way." The users who would have access to the API could also be limited, and a limit could be set to the number of molecules a user could generate at once. Still, Ben Ouagrham-Gormley contends that without showing that the technology could readily foster bioweapon development, such regulation could be premature.

For their part, Urbina and Ekins view their work as a first step in drawing attention to the issue of misuse of this technology. "We don't want to portray these things as being bad because they actually do have a lot of value," Ekins says. "But there is that dark side to it. There is that note of caution, and I think it is important to consider that."

About the Author

Rebecca Sohn is a freelance health and science journalist based in New York City. She has written for outlets such as Slate, Spectrum, STAT *and* Live Science, *among others.*

Is Bird Flu Waiting to Explode?

By Fred Guterl

The chickens were already getting sick when Yoshihiro Kawaoka arrived in the U.S. in August 1983. A few months before, in April, a bird flu virus had arisen in the poultry farms of eastern Pennsylvania, but veterinarians had deemed it to be "low pathogenic"—meaning it made chickens sick but did not kill many of them. As the virus swept through the poultry farms, however, a new strain developed. Chickens began to die in large numbers, and farmers started to fear for their livelihoods. The state called in the U.S. Department of Agriculture, which set up a temporary command and control center in a strip mall outside of Lancaster. To contain the epidemic, it culled 17 million birds from Pennsylvania down through Virginia.

Kawaoka was a young researcher from Japan who was starting work at St. Jude Children's Research Hospital in Memphis. His boss, virologist Robert Webster, had a theory that human influenza viruses originate in bird populations—that they circulate harmlessly among ducks and geese and that, every once in a while, a strain will evolve the ability to live in the human upper respiratory tract. To combat human influenza, Webster asserted, you first had to understand bird flu. In November, when Webster heard that the outbreak had become serious, he dropped everything and headed to its epicenter.

Kawaoka stayed behind and watched the crisis unfold from behind the air lock of the Memphis hospital's biocontainment laboratory. He took samples sent back to him from the field, extracted the virus and cultured it. He then infected chickens that he kept in cages along a wall and waited to see what happened. What he found disturbed him: each and every chicken died—a mortality rate of 100 percent. In autopsies, he found that the virus was a ruthless pathogen, attacking almost every organ—similar to what some strains of Ebola do to humans.

In the months after the crisis, Kawaoka puzzled over why the April strain of the virus was so mild and why the strain that it evolved into by November was so deadly. He decided to compare the two. The difference, he discovered, came down to relatively small changes in the virus. "What this tells you," Kawaoka told me in an interview in 2010, "is that a highly pathogenic virus was generated from a single mutation. And it tells you there are many sources of highly pathogenic influenza viruses. It's all out there in birds."

The experience brought home to Kawaoka the urgency for scientists to figure out how bird flu can cause trouble for humans–the better to detect it early or to prepare effective vaccines and treatments. In particular, he wanted to know if a lethal bird flu akin to the one that burned through poultry farms in 1983 could turn into a human disease. And if so, what sequence of genetic code would the virus have to acquire?

Nearly three decades later Kawaoka got an answer. He took an avian flu–an H5N1 type–that lives in birds and combined it with the H1N1 pandemic virus of 2009. Then he tested his hybrid virus on ferrets–a common research stand-in for humans–and found that it spread easily by airborne droplets. With this result, the notion that an H5N1 influenza virus could become a human pathogen was no longer hypothetical. If he could do it in a lab, nature could do it, too.

Kawaoka submitted his paper to the journal *Nature*, which then sent it out to his peers for review, a standard practice. (*Scientific American* is part of Nature Publishing Group.) Virologist Ron Fouchier of Erasmus Medical Center in Rotterdam also independently concocted a potentially human transmissible H5N1 virus and tested it on ferrets; he submitted his paper to the journal *Science*. At some point, the White House got wind of the studies. By December 2011 biosecurity officials were pushing for a delay in publication and a moratorium on the research.

What had biosecurity experts worried is that one of these viruses could possibly do to people what the 1983 virus did to chickens. If that were the case, the research might serve as a blueprint for a bioweapon. Or perhaps the virus itself could escape from a lab via a worker who became infected accidentally. For the months after the submission of the papers, scientists argued publicly and often vociferously with one another about whether the new viruses were potentially lethal and what kinds of restraints, if any, should be applied to work on H5N1 influenza viruses. The practice of science, which thrives on the free flow of information and the propensity of scientists to follow their curiosity wherever it may lead, collided with the need to keep people safe from a pathogen that could arguably be considered a potential weapon of mass destruction–every bit as devastating, and troublesome to manage, as nuclear weapons.

The Natural Threat

The first recorded instance of a "fowl plague" on poultry farms occurred in the countryside of northern Italy in 1878. It was thought to be a particularly virulent form of cholera. By 1901 scientists had pegged it to a virus of some kind. By 1955 they realized it was type A influenza, similar to strains that infect humans, which later led Webster and others to wonder if there was some relation between influenza in birds and human outbreaks.

Webster's hunch about birds being a reservoir for precursors to human viruses is now conventional wisdom. Wild birds carry such viruses around in their gastrointestinal tract without becoming sick and transmit the virus through feces. If a wild bird infects a chicken on a poultry farm, the virus may get opportunities to interact with a range of additional viruses through close contact with pigs and other animals. This is indeed what has happened in the live animal markets and backyard farms of China and southern Asia. Influenza viruses are notorious for their ability to change, through a combination of mutation and "reassortment"–a borrowing of genes from other viruses. An open farm acts like a virus convention, where different strains swap genetic material like conventioneers swap business cards.

In the past few decades influenza specialists have focused their worry on the H5N1 strains circulating on Asian farms.

Type A influenza viruses are categorized by their surface proteins hemagglutinin and neuraminidase–the "H" and "N" in the species designations. (The 1983 virus was an H5N2.) If a virus can be said to have a personality, the H5N1 virus seems restless and unpredictable. For instance, the virus was thought to be benign in wild birds, but in 2005 thousands of ducks, geese, gulls and cormorants were found dead in Qinghai Lake in Central China, apparently killed by H5N1. In the past decade H5N1 has killed civets in Vietnam and tigers in a Thai zoo.

It has killed people, too. During the outbreak among poultry in Asia in 1997, a three-year-old boy in Hong Kong became the first known human fatality. By year's end the death toll was six. To stem the outbreak, authorities in China and neighboring countries oversaw the culling of millions of birds. Still, the virus came surging back in 2004 in Thailand, Vietnam, China and Indonesia.

All told, around 350 people have died from H5N1, most from contact with birds. The absolute number is not high, but the virus, according to the World Health Organization, has a mortality rate of about 60 percent. In contrast, the 1918 influenza virus, which killed 20 million to 50 million people, had a mortality rate of about 2 percent. Since the Kawaoka and Fouchier papers surfaced last fall, the actual mortality rate of H5N1 has been the subject of intense debate. Some scientists–notably, Peter Palese, professor of infectious diseases and chair of microbiology at the Mount Sinai School of Medicine–argue that mild cases of H5N1 have gone underreported or do not register in tests, which has artificially driven up the mortality rate. Others argue that deaths from H5N1 have gone underreported, which may make the mortality rate appear lower than it actually is. Kawaoka and Fouchier have reported low mortality among ferrets for their lab-made viruses. Whatever the danger these particular viruses might or might not pose, the fact that H5N1 could potentially spread easily among humans is not good news.

In September 2001 anthrax that had been weaponized as a fine white powder made its way through the U.S. mail, killing five people and terrorizing a nation already skittish from the World Trade Center and Pentagon attacks on 9/11. Spending on biodefense soared. Since 2001 the U.S. government has plowed more than $60 billion into vaccine stockpiling, disease surveillance and basic research into potential bioweapons agents, including influenza. The National Institute of Allergy and Infectious Disease (NIAID), the major source of funds in the U.S., nearly tripled its budget on influenza research in fiscal year 2003–from $17 million to $50 million–and doubled it again to $100 million in 2004. In 2009 funding hit a peak of nearly $300 million, from which it has come down slightly. Kawaoka was the recipient of some of that largesse. Since 2006 he has received nearly $500,000 a year from NIAID for research on the "pandemic potential of H5N1 influenza viruses," according to the National Institutes of Health Web site. Fouchier got his funding from Palese's group at Mount Sinai, which subcontracted the work from a grant from NIAID. Fouchier's lab made mutations to an H5N1 virus to enhance transmissibility and then passed the virus to ferrets until it spread via airborne droplets among them. The Centers of Disease Control and Prevention also had a group investigating transmissibility of H5N1, but it was not as successful as Kawaoka's and Fouchier's groups.

The Weapon

For years after 9/11, however, concerns over smallpox as a potential bioweapon eclipsed those of influenza. The variola virus that causes smallpox kills one in three people infected and persists for years between hosts. It was declared eradicated in 1979. Although officially only two samples are kept under lock and key in Atlanta and in Koltsovo, Russia, there have been persistent rumors of other, illicit samples. In response to heightened fears after the 9/11 attacks, the U.S. stockpiled about 300,000 doses of smallpox vaccine, which now sit in secret warehouses throughout the country.

Influenza made it onto the bioweapons agenda in 2005, but biosecurity officials gave it a pass. Scientists had succeeded in reconstructing the 1918 pandemic flu virus from tissue samples of human remains that had been frozen in Arctic ice. The National Science Advisory Board for Biosecurity (NSABB) conferred and decided that the benefits to science and public health outweighed the security risk. Current NSABB chair Paul Keim recently called that decision "a mistake." The 2009 pandemic virus, an H1N1 type with low pathogenicity, made the issue moot by conferring at least partial immunity to the 1918 virus to much of the world's population. Since H5N1 is novel to the human immune system, there is no natural resistance.

Some defense experts now consider Kawaoka's and Fouchier's lab-made H5N1 viruses to be potentially more dangerous than smallpox. Influenza viruses are more contagious than variola and move more quickly through human populations, which gives public health officials less time to marshal vaccines and treatments. "Influenza is the lion king of transmissibility," says Michael Osterholm, director of the Center for Infectious Disease Research and Policy at the University of Minnesota and an outspoken member of the NSABB. A highly transmissible H5N1 virus with a human mortality rate even approaching the 60 percent observed so far among bird flu victims is a terrifying prospect. As Osterholm has pointed out, even at one-twentieth the pathogenicity, H5N1 would be deadlier than the 1918 pandemic virus. NSABB called for a withholding of details in the Kawaoka and Fouchier papers last December but gave the go-ahead for full publication in March.

There is general agreement in the biosecurity community that bird flu—or, to be specific, H5N1 viruses made in the laboratory to be transmissible among mammals—is a potential bioweapon, which, like smallpox, has to be managed. "The very fact that this virus exists creates a risk," says Richard H. Ebright, a biodefense expert and chemical biologist at Rutgers University. "It creates the risk of accidental release, and it creates the risk that someone will turn it into a weapon."

What has defense experts, as well as many scientists, miffed is that the research proceeded without any analysis of the benefits and the risks beforehand. The NSABB, purely an advisory board with no oversight responsibility, got involved only after prodding by the White House. In 2007 John Steinbruner and his colleagues at the Center for International and Security Studies at Maryland wrote a report recommending "some constraint on freedom of action at the level of fundamental research, where individual autonomy has traditionally been highly valued for the best of reasons." The report was largely ignored. After the Fouchier and Kawaoka papers came to light, however, the U.S. government called on funding agencies to perform risk assessments on research involving the H5N1 and 1918 flu viruses.

Steinbruner and others recommend some kind of international oversight group with some power to impose mandatory constraints on potentially dangerous research and oversee it, much as the WHO does now with smallpox. "It wouldn't be an airtight protection, but it would establish the norm that nobody can go off into a closet and do these experiments," Steinbruner says. An H5N1 virus engineered to spread among mammals "is an agent of mass destruction that gets into the nuclear weapons league and even exceeds it," he adds. "It is a very dangerous pathogen. It's not a matter of [scientists] being personally careful. There's got to be some institutional safety procedure."

How restrictive should those procedures be? Nuclear weapons technology is subject to military classification, which means some research can only be conducted in secret. Unlike nuclear weapons, however, influenza is a matter of global public health. Classifying some aspects of H5N1 research would leave scientists and health officials in the dark about one of the world's bigger public health threats. In contrast, many security experts argue in favor of restricting research on mammal-transmissible viruses to only the most secure labs—more secure than the labs Kawaoka and Fouchier did their work in. Such restrictions would put the research out of reach of many scientists.

Many investigators have been passionate in their defense of the kind of work Kawaoka and Fouchier have done on the grounds that the more we know about H5N1, the better we can protect ourselves from the natural threat. Science, the argument goes, advances best when research activities are unfettered. Pinning down precisely what genetic components are needed to confer traits such as lethality and transmissibility on H5N1 would allow health experts to be on the watch for dangerous new strains that emerge in the wild and prepare for them in advance. Once a novel human flu virus crops up and begins to spread, it is too late to stop the first wave of infection. Flu vaccine production typically takes six months to complete, sometimes more. For instance, by the time the H1N1 virus came to the attention of health officials in April 2009, it had spread widely in Mexico and the U.S. and was well on its way to becoming a pandemic.

Moreover, one of the genetic components Kawaoka identified as conferring transmissibility on H5N1 has been observed in natural viruses, which suggests that the roulette wheel is already in spin. "Because H5N1 mutations that confer transmissibility in mammals may emerge in nature, I believe that it would be irresponsible not to study the underlying mechanism," Kawaoka wrote in an essay in Nature. (He declined to be interviewed for this article.) Fouchier has defended his work on the same grounds.

Having the genetic details of potentially deadly flu viruses is of little use, however, without the funding, networks and access to animals out in the field. During the H5N1 outbreaks, virologists began rigorous monitoring of the live animal markets in southern China, but those measures have not been applied consistently elsewhere in China or Southeast Asia. In the U.S., livestock farms often bar health officials from testing their pigs even though precursors of the 2009 H1N1 pandemic are thought to have kicked around U.S. pig farms for years before emerging in Mexico

Surveillance may never be good enough to forestall human pandemics. "We're better prepared now than we were prior to the H1N1 pandemic," says Nancy Cox, director of the Influenza Division of the CDC, "but the world is not prepared for the emergence of highly transmissible, highly pathogenic influenza virus in humans. Honestly, I don't think the world ever will be unless we have a universal vaccine that protects against all strains." A universal vaccine is not in sight, which leaves us in the uncomfortable position of having too much knowledge and too little.

About the Author

Fred Guterl is executive editor of Scientific American *and author of* The Fate of the Species *(Bloomsbury, 2012).*

Section 4: Science Fiction or Military Fact?

The Physics and Hype of Hypersonic Weapons

By David Wright and Cameron Tracy

In a televised address to Russia's Federal Assembly in 2018, President Vladimir Putin announced an escalation of the ongoing arms race with the U.S., which had withdrawn from the Anti-Ballistic Missile (ABM) Treaty in 2002. Having rejected the decades-long arms-control agreement, the U.S. had developed and begun building a network of defenses to intercept long-range ballistic missiles, threatening Russia's ability to deter attacks on its homeland. He had warned Americans that Russia would be forced to respond to these deployments, Putin told his audience, but they had refused to listen. "So listen now!"

Among other systems, Russia was developing new hypersonic weapons, Putin declared: missiles that fly long distances through the atmosphere at more than five times the speed of sound, or faster than Mach 5. (Mach 1 is the local speed of sound. Speeds between Mach 1 and Mach 5 are supersonic, whereas those exceeding Mach 5 are hypersonic.) According to him, one of these, called Avangard, was a highly maneuverable missile that could glide thousands of kilometers with an initial speed greater than Mach 20, making it "absolutely invulnerable to any air or missile defense system."

Putin's announcement, accompanied by intimidating simulations of the new weapons snaking across the globe at unbelievable speeds, added fuel to a dangerous new arms race. The weapons involved in this competition are touted not only for their speed but also for their stealth and maneuverability. Intercontinental ballistic missiles, which follow an elliptical path into space before plunging down toward their target, reach speeds above Mach 20, but they have predictable trajectories for most of their flight and typically can maneuver only briefly, after they reenter the atmosphere. In contrast, hypersonic weapons would fly deep within the atmosphere most of the time, using lift generated by airflow to weave around and try to evade interceptors. Approaching at such low altitudes, these weapons would avoid detection by ground-based radar systems until close to their target, making them more difficult to stop.

In an assessment after Putin's speech, U.S. military officials stated that hypersonic weapons, which China was also developing, would "revolutionize warfare." The Pentagon, which had been working on similar systems for a decade and a half, ramped up its own efforts; last year Congress dedicated $3.2 billion to the research and development of hypersonic weapons and defenses. Russia and China now claim to each have deployed at least one such system. The U.S. has six known hypersonic programs, divided among the air force, army and navy. Proponents say that these weapons are incredibly fast and agile and virtually invisible.

We disagree. We belong to a small but vibrant community of physicists and engineers scattered around the globe who study new weapons systems to understand their potential impacts on global security. This tradition is deep, going back to participants in the Manhattan Project and Russian scientists such as Andrei Sakharov, who sought to mitigate the danger to the world from the nuclear weapons they had helped create. As investigative physicists, we glean what information we can about new and usually secretive technologies, analyze it and share our evaluations with the public.

Our studies indicate that hypersonic weapons may have advantages in certain scenarios, but by no means do they constitute a revolution. Many of the claims about them are exaggerated or simply false. And yet the widespread perception that hypersonic weapons are a game-changer has increased tensions among the U.S., Russia and China, driving a new arms race and escalating the chances of conflict.

Fits and Starts

Militaries have pursued hypersonic aircraft for almost a century, though with limited success. In the late 1930s Austrian engineer

Eugen Sänger and German physicist Irene Bredt designed the first hypersonic aircraft, a glider called the Silbervogel. It was to be launched from a rocket, fly primarily within the atmosphere and, like any other glider, stay aloft using aerodynamic lift, but Nazi planners decided it would be too difficult and expensive to build.

During World War II, German engineers developed rocket engines, which burn propellant, a mixture of fuel and chemical oxidizer, to release an intense burst of energy. In subsequent decades, experimental rocket-powered aircraft broke speed record after speed record. In October 1947 the rocket-propelled X-1 became the first piloted aircraft to officially break the sound barrier—crossing Mach 1—and in the 1960s the X-15 reached Mach 6.7 during tests. The strong g-forces produced by rocket engines placed extreme demands on human physiology, so piloted rocket-propelled aircraft never became more than experiments. But rocket technology enabled the U.S. and the Soviet Union to build arsenals of nuclear-armed ballistic missiles that are boosted to more than Mach 20 to reach across continents.

Another technology developed in this era, the jet engine, became the workhorse of military and commercial travel, however. Drawing in atmospheric oxygen to continuously burn fuel, a jet engine does not carry the extra weight of an oxidizer. It enables long-distance transport and maneuverability without the extreme acceleration of rocket engines. Today the fastest official speed for a piloted jet aircraft stands at approximately Mach 3, which the Lockheed SR-71 Blackbird reached in July 1976. Jet engines also power cruise missiles—maneuverable and pilotless aircraft, the fastest of which can achieve supersonic speeds.

Meanwhile hypersonic gliders continued to soar—and drop. In 1963, after spending over $5 billion (in current dollars) developing the X-20 Dyna-Soar hypersonic glider, the U.S. abandoned the design. But after the Al Qaeda attacks on September 11, 2001, President George W. Bush directed the development of hypersonic missiles that could quickly and accurately disrupt terrorist activities on different continents with nonnuclear warheads. (Ballistic missiles could do the job, but the launch of such a weapon could be mistaken for a nuclear attack, provoking a nuclear war.)

Bush also withdrew from the Anti-Ballistic Missile treaty, which the U.S. and the Soviet Union had signed in 1972. The treaty had stopped the adversaries from constructing defensive shields against each other's ballistic missiles—and thereby halted a race for technologies to build shields and break through those of the other side. Instead the Bush administration proceeded to develop and deploy interceptors to protect against long-range ballistic missiles. Fearing that their ability to deter a U.S. nuclear attack would be compromised, Russia and, more recently, China, began to pursue diverse stratagems for surmounting the U.S. shield. The most recent of these devices are hypersonic missiles, which fly too low to be blocked by current U.S. interceptors of long-range ballistic missiles. In sum, the 9/11 attacks provoked a series of hasty decisions that have brought the three superpowers to the present situation, in which they are all racing to develop hypersonic weapons based on various technologies and designed for various purposes.

Drag and Lift

Hypersonic systems deployed in the near term will be "boost-glide" weapons, which would be launched by a rocket booster and then glide long distances without propulsion. (The U.S. and other countries are also working to build hypersonic cruise missiles, but their engines are still under development.) Yet our studies indicate that hypersonic gliders encounter severe challenges. Physics gets in the way.

Designers of hypersonic vehicles face a daunting adversary: drag, the resistance a fluid offers to anything moving through it. The drag on a flying object increases in proportion to the square of its velocity, making it particularly debilitating at hypersonic speeds. A glider at Mach 5 is subjected to 25 times the drag force than when it flies at Mach 1, for example, and one at Mach 20 faces 400 times the drag of when it is at Mach 1.

Even more severe is the energy drain from an aircraft as it pushes the molecules of air forward and aside: it increases as the cube of the velocity. So a glider flying at Mach 5 will lose energy 125 times faster than at Mach 1; one flying at Mach 20 will lose energy 8,000 times faster. Just as problematic, the kinetic energy flowing from the glider to the surrounding air transforms to thermal energy and shock waves. Some of that energy transfers back to the vehicle as heat: leading edges of boost-glide weapons flying at Mach 10 or above can reach temperatures above 2,000 kelvins for sustained periods. Protecting a vehicle from this intense heat is one of the biggest problems facing engineers.

At the same time, like any other glider, a hypersonic one must generate lift–a force perpendicular to its direction of motion–to stay aloft and to turn. (A glider turns by banking or otherwise inducing a horizontal component of the lift force.) As it happens, lift is also proportional to the square of the velocity. Moreover, the aerodynamic processes that produce lift also unavoidably generate drag. The ratio of the lift force, L, to the drag force, D, is called the lift-to-drag ratio, L/D, a key marker of a glider's performance.

Achievable values of L/D for hypersonic vehicles are much lower than for conventional aircraft. For subsonic aircraft, the ratio can be 15 or larger. Yet after decades of research and development, U.S. hypersonic weapons tested in the past decade appear to have L/D values less than three. Such low L/D ratios mean low lift and high drag–which limits the speed and range of a hypersonic glider, reduces its maneuverability and increases surface heating.

As if that were not enough, the physics and chemistry of air flowing past an object become radically different at hypersonic speeds. Heated to thousands of degrees, the surrounding air dissociates, converting molecular oxygen into free atoms that can ionize and scour away the surface of the vehicle. Even if the missile survives the roasting, the heating produces a bright infrared signal that satellites can see.

No Silver Bullet

In the early 2010s the U.S. flight-tested a long-range glider, the Hypersonic Technology Vehicle 2 (HTV-2). It was designed to glide up to 7,600 kilometers after being boosted to an initial speed of Mach 20 by a rocket. We combined data from these tests with other information about the vehicle to construct detailed computer simulations of hypersonic flight. We also compared the performance of boost-glide weapons with long-established technologies, such as ballistic or cruise missiles, on the three abilities in which hypersonic weapons are said to be exceptional–delivery time, maneuverability and stealth.

Hypersonic weapons are often said to reduce the time needed to deliver a warhead, but this claim is largely based on a misleading comparison with subsonic cruise missiles or with ballistic missiles on longer trajectories. The most energy-efficient path for a ballistic missile, called a minimum-energy trajectory, sends a warhead arcing high above Earth before it falls to its target. The warhead avoids atmospheric drag over most of its flight but follows a much longer path than a hypersonic glider would, so it can take somewhat longer to reach the same target.

Yet a ballistic missile can instead fly at lower altitude, called a depressed trajectory–long seen as a way of delivering quicker nuclear attacks from submarines. Such a path would be much shorter than a minimum-energy one, and a warhead following it would also avoid drag over most of its trajectory. In contrast, a hypersonic glider spends significantly more time within the atmosphere, where drag reduces its speed. Our calculations show that a ballistic missile on a depressed trajectory can deliver a warhead with an equal or shorter flight time than a hypersonic weapon over the same range.

Maneuvering is another advertised advantage of hypersonic weapons. Again, the reality is more complicated. The U.S. has developed and tested maneuvering reentry vehicles (MaRVs)–warheads that use aerodynamic forces to change direction as they near the target, helping to increase accuracy and evade missile defenses–for ballistic missiles for decades: maneuverability is not unique to hypersonic weapons. To be sure, MaRVs typically twist and turn only late in flight. They cannot snake around during their entire course as hypersonic gliders are supposed to do. But the maneuverability of hypersonic gliders is constrained by the great forces needed to turn a vehicle flying at such tremendous speeds.

To change direction, a hypersonic glider must use lift forces to impart a horizontal velocity–which might itself have to be hypersonic. For example, to turn by 30 degrees, a glider flying at Mach 15, or 4.5 kilometers per second, must generate a horizontal velocity of Mach 7.5, or 2.3 kilometers per second. (Because the speed of sound changes with density and altitude, flight engineers often take Mach 1 to be about 300 meters per second, and so do we.) At the same time, the glider must retain enough vertical lift to stay aloft. Such maneuvers can cost significant speed and range.

To generate the extra lift needed to change direction, the vehicle could dive to a lower altitude to use the greater push from denser air. It would make its turn before returning to a higher altitude, with less drag, to resume its flight. Going to lower altitudes would reduce the time needed to turn but also increase the drag that the vehicle experiences. For example, at Mach 15 a glider such as the HTV-2 would fly at an altitude of about 40 kilometers. If it drops by about 2.5 kilometers, then turning by 30 degrees would take about seven minutes, during which it would travel along a vast arc, with a radius of some 4,000 kilometers. The extra drag that comes from traveling in denser air, even for such a short time, would reduce the glider's speed by about Mach 1.3, causing it to lose about 450 kilometers of range out of the 3,000 kilometers it might otherwise have traveled.

Some amount of midcourse maneuvering, such as for selecting a new target, can be useful, and gliders could likely make larger maneuvers than ballistic missile warheads can. Still, MaRVs can already maneuver by hundreds of kilometers during reentry, so it is hard to see how this ability is revolutionary.

Another common claim is that because gliders travel at lower altitudes than a ballistic warhead, they would be "nearly invisible" to early-warning systems. A ground-based radar system can spot a warhead at an altitude of 1,000 kilometers from about 3,500 kilometers away, but because of the earth's curvature it would not see a glider approaching at a height of 40 kilometers until it was only about 500 kilometers away. But both the U.S. and Russia have early-warning satellites with sensitive infrared sensors that could spot the intense light that gliders emit because of their extreme temperatures. Our analysis indicates that currently deployed U.S. satellites would be capable of detecting and tracking gliders traveling through the atmosphere at speeds covering most of the hypersonic regime.

Gliders deployable in the foreseeable future might avoid being seen by U.S. satellites if they fly at the low end of the hypersonic range– below about Mach 6. This concern appears to be motivating U.S. research into new constellations of satellite sensors. But a boost-glide vehicle similar to the HTV-2 with an initial speed of Mach 5.5 would travel less than 500 kilometers, so flying at these speeds would significantly limit its range. Hypersonic cruise missiles could conceivably maintain these low speeds over longer distances. Such slow speeds may, however, negate another key argument for hypersonic weapons–their ability to avoid terminal missile defenses.

Russia and China seem to be developing hypersonic weapons largely because of their ability to evade U.S. missile defense systems. The U.S. Ground-based Midcourse Defense and ship-based Aegis SM-3 systems, which are intended to defend the U.S., Japan, and other countries, intercept above the atmosphere and are unable to engage hypersonic weapons flying in at lower altitudes. Hypersonic gliders with sufficient speed and maneuverability could also evade defenses of shorter range that work within the atmosphere, such as the U.S. Patriot, SM-2 and THAAD systems. These interceptors protect small regions, tens of kilometers across, around military sites and ships, using lift forces for turning to intercept incoming weapons. Their efficacy depends on their being more maneuverable than the missile they are trying to hit, which in turn depends strongly on flight speed. Patriot interceptors, for example, use rocket boosters to reach speeds of up to Mach 6. A hypersonic weapon could likely outmaneuver these interceptors if it maintained high speeds–but could become vulnerable to them when flying below about Mach 6. Thus, almost as soon as a hypersonic glider becomes invisible to satellites (but possibly visible to ground radar), it can become susceptible to interception.

Moreover, the ability to penetrate defensive shields is not unique to hypersonic gliders. Interceptors that operate outside the atmosphere are particularly vulnerable to being fooled by decoys and other countermeasures, which Russia and China have developed and likely deployed. Ballistic missiles of short and medium range, launched from an aircraft, could fly at altitudes low enough to avoid such "exo-atmospheric" defenses. Similarly, equipping ballistic missiles, including missiles of short and medium range, with MaRVs could allow them to outmaneuver and penetrate defenses that operate within the atmosphere.

Today the U.S. has shifted its focus from developing long-range gliders such as the HTV-2 toward hypersonic systems of shorter range, of up to a few thousand kilometers. This change is motivated not only by the shortcomings of the prototype HTV-2 glider, which the tests had revealed, but also by a new mission: to use weapons in a local, or "theater," conflict to penetrate and destroy defensive systems. In terms of capabilities, however, these shorter-range hypersonic gliders are virtually indistinguishable from MaRV-tipped ballistic missiles flying on depressed trajectories. The similarity became obvious in 2018, when the U.S. Department of Defense announced its choice of design for a hypersonic vehicle intended for joint use by the army, navy and air force. Rather than opting for a wedge shape like that of the HTV-2, which would increase the value of L/D, the Pentagon chose an older conical design based on an experimental MaRV originally developed in the 1970s. This weapon would have a lower range and less maneuverability, the Pentagon acknowledged, but the technology was less risky.

A design from the 1970s is hardly revolutionary. It looks to us like the Pentagon is using the hype about hypersonic weapons to secure funding from Congress while reverting to a technology developed half a century ago for its main system. While the Pentagon is putting some funds into other designs, its focus is not the revolutionary systems that were advertised.

Waverider

Significantly enhancing L/D, if possible, would reduce the technical barriers to long-range hypersonic flight. Theoretically, "waverider" designs can increase the L/D values of hypersonic vehicles to six or higher. These use a wedge shape that matches the shock-wave pattern of the airflow around the glider at a given speed and altitude, enclosing part of the shock wave under the vehicle to provide additional lift.

This concept dates from the late 1950s but has proved difficult to transform into working vehicles. The HTV-2 was in fact based on such a design—but achieved an L/D value of only 2.6. Even so, in 2020 the air force withdrew from the Pentagon's joint hypersonic program and announced that it would pursue a wedge design like that of the HTV-2 for a short-range glider. Increasing L/D to four or six would help reduce heat loads and increase a glider's range. But would such improvements open new possibilities for military uses?

We think not. Heating remains a major challenge because the surface temperature of a vehicle falls rather slowly with increases in L/D. Our calculations show, for example, that increasing L/D from 2.6, the value that the HTV-2 achieved, to 6 would reduce a glider's surface temperature at a given speed by at most 15 percent. Preventing material damage during long-range flights would therefore still be difficult. Such an increase in L/D would also reduce the infrared signature of a missile and potentially increase the speed at which it could fly undetected (by current satellites) to up to Mach 7. Increasing L/D could in addition provide somewhat higher maneuverability—but that could be more easily boosted by relatively small increases in a glider's initial speed. (Recall that maneuverability depends on lift, which increases as the square of the velocity.) For such reasons, it does not look like foreseeable advances in hypersonic gliders, such as increasing L/D, would give hypersonic weapons revolutionary capabilities.

Despite this reality, the hype around hypersonic weapons has driven big increases in spending on these systems and heightened fear, distrust and the risk of conflict among the U.S., Russia and China. The prospect of fast and potentially undetected attacks, even if exaggerated, could prompt these countries to react quickly and rashly to warnings, either real or mistaken, increasing the chances of blundering into conflict.

By providing technical analyses of new military systems, independent scientists and engineers such as ourselves seek to help the public and policy makers make sound decisions about them. Our ranks are thinning, however. Although funds for designing and building novel weapons seem inexhaustible, resources for such impartial research into their abilities and impacts is shrinking—creating daunting barriers for early-career researchers who might otherwise be inclined to join the field. We believe that the unbiased and informed studies we provide are vital, however, and policy makers should heed them. The U.S. Congress and the Pentagon need to dispense with the hype and make a careful, realistic and technically informed appraisal of the potential benefits and costs of hypersonic weapons. Failure to fully assess these factors is a recipe for wasteful spending and increased global risk.

About the Authors

David Wright is a research affiliate at the Laboratory for Nuclear Security and Policy at the Massachusetts Institute of Technology. He formerly co-directed the Global Security Program at the Union of Concerned Scientists.

Cameron Tracy is a Global Security Fellow at the Union of Concerned Scientists. An engineer and materials scientist, he researches hypersonic weapons and nuclear waste management.

Hypersonic Weapons Can't Hide from New Eyes in Space

By Jason Sherman

China's test flight of a long-range hypersonic glide vehicle late last year was described in the media as close to a "Sputnik moment" in the race to develop new ultrafast maneuvering weapons. But even as senior U.S. military officials publicly fretted about missiles that are, for the moment at least, effectively invincible, the Pentagon was quietly making strides on an entirely novel way to help shoot down these weapons.

Late last December the U.S. Department of Defense's Missile Defense Agency (MDA) gave the green light to a pair of contractors—L3Harris Technologies and Northrop Grumman—to pivot from design to prototype fabrication of a Hypersonic and Ballistic Tracking Space Sensor (HBTSS) system. This technology is intended to solve one of the Pentagon's most vexing technical challenges: how to detect and track the hypersonic glide vehicles that exploit blind spots in today's radar networks.

Both Russia and China have fielded hypersonic glide vehicles, in 2019 and 2020 respectively, but the U.S. is not expected to deploy a comparable offensive weapon until 2023. In contrast to ballistic missile payload trajectories, hypersonic glide vehicles can maneuver on the way to a target. This makes it extremely difficult to track them. These weapons start their journey when a large rocket boosts them to an altitude near the edge of space and releases them. Then the glide vehicles divert to a flatter trajectory—either exiting the atmosphere or staying just within it—and sail on unpowered. They use aerodynamic lift to skip across the atmosphere to their targets at hypersonic speeds. This near-space trajectory and the ability to shift course let hypersonic glide vehicles evade the combination of space and terrestrial sensors used to track ballistic missiles. The Pentagon can detect the launch—but the hypersonic glide vehicle then slips out of view until late in the weapon's flight because of ground radar's line-of-sight limitations. As a result, defensive systems have little, if any, time left to halt an incoming weapon.

HBTSS is intended to solve this problem by continuously tracking long-range missiles from launch to impact. It will also have the ability to hand off critical information to ships, aircraft and ground forces, enabling them to fire their own missiles at incoming threats. The detection system relies on a new network of orbiting sensors, a critical part of a dense and multilayered constellation of satellites the Pentagon has already begun placing in low-earth orbit. Experimental and prototype payloads were sent into orbit last June, and initial operational payloads are slated for launch in 2022 and 2023. These sensors detect heat signatures to identify missile launches and will give the U.S. military the ability to track targets, described as cradle-to-grave target custody.

Some of the pivotal components of HBTSS are "signal to clutter" algorithms designed to distinguish a fast-moving threat from the warm and irregular surface of Earth. This is a much more difficult task than that of ground radar, which tracks missiles as they move across the cold and featureless background of the sky. "Just imagine a light bulb moving across a background of light bulbs, and you have to pick out that light bulb," says Paul Wloszek, director of missile defense at L3Harris Space & Airborne Systems. "You have to know where it's at–and how fast it's going–to be able to shoot it down."

To address this problem, in October 2019 the Pentagon separately tapped L3Harris and Northrop Grumman (and two other companies subsequently bumped from the competition) to develop tracking algorithms sensitive enough to distinguish the signal from the noise. In late 2020 L3Harris and Northrop Grumman paired their respective algorithms with compact, powerful computer processors small enough to be incorporated into space vehicles. Both companies performed a successful "signal chain demonstration," which proved their systems' ability to detect and track dim targets against a cluttered background. The signal chain demonstration verified the sensitivity necessary to support the so-called hypersonic kill chain—the discrete actions required in sequence between identifying and striking a target.

Other space-based assets already provide the U.S. with overhead infrared sensing. But the key characteristic that sets HBTSS apart is a requirement to generate what the Pentagon calls "fire control quality" tracking data. This is very precise information that can be used by terrestrial command-and-control systems to steer guided-missile interceptors against hypersonic threats.

"Being able to see down from space, warm tracks going over a warm Earth—that is really tough science," said MDA director Vice Admiral Jon Hill at a hearing of the Senate Committee on Armed Service's Subcommittee on Strategic Forces late last spring. "But we've got that licked. We've shown that we can do that on the ground. That sort of capability gives us global coverage."

On December 27 President Joe Biden signed the National Defense Authorization Act for Fiscal Year 2022, which includes $256 million for HBTSS. The funding will support continued development of the tracking algorithms, as well as beginning the assembly of infrared sensors bound for launch in 2023. Both L3Harris and Northrop Grumman are set to deliver two HBTSS prototypes each, including software and hardware. Congress, however, is currently at an impasse over fiscal year 2022 appropriations. If the government cannot reach an agreement, HBTSS could be limited to 2021 spending levels for the project: $130 million, a sum that would likely imperil the project's schedule. In that case, the Pentagon could stitch together existing systems to deliver something HBTSS-like, says hypersonics expert David Wright, a research affiliate at the Massachusetts Institute of Technology's Laboratory for Nuclear Security and Policy.

"HBTSS would be nice to have, but it's not clear to me that it gives you unique capabilities," Wright says. He explains that the capabilities promised by HBTSS could also be achieved without a new space-based program by relying on ground sensors placed in the correct locations. This might involve carefully positioning ships equipped with powerful radar in order to expand defensive zones. "I think it's a system I can imagine the military wanting because they'd like to be able to track these systems continually—and it could do that tracking outside of the [ground] radar range—but I'm not convinced that that's necessary," Wright adds.

Victoria Samson, a military space expert at the Secure World Foundation, agrees there is a need to track advanced threats across their entire flight path but notes that advocates of HBTSS may be underestimating the task of dealing with this high-profile challenge. "I think it's a lot more complicated than the supporters would let on, and adding hypersonic to the [operations] requirement may be more a nod to its increased visibility among national security folks than anything else," Samson says.

Along with sensors, the Pentagon is thinking anew about the guided missiles needed to defeat hypersonic glide vehicles. In late May 2021 the MDA revealed it had certified the currently deployed Standard Missile-6 as a last line of defense for aircraft carrier strike groups to use against hypersonic glide vehicles. And in November 2021 MDA tapped three companies to advance designs for a new weapon, called a Glide Phase Interceptor, intended to counter hypersonic threats. This sets up a three-way contest between Lockheed Martin, Raytheon and Northrop Grumman to field a new weapon within the decade.

About the Author

Jason Sherman is an investigative national security reporter with more than 25 years of experience covering the Pentagon, the military budget, weapon system acquisition and defense policy formulation, along with technology, business and global arms trade. He has traveled to more than 40 countries, studied medieval history at the State University of New York at Buffalo, and lives in Brooklyn, N.Y.

How Do We Prevent War in Space?

By Ann Finkbeiner

On January 30, 2020, an amateur satellite watcher tweeted, "Something to potentially watch." Cosmos 2542, a Russian inspection satellite, was "loitering around" USA 245, an American spy satellite, and, he wrote, "as I'm typing this, that offset distance shifts between 150 and 300 kilometers." USA 245 then adjusted its orbit to get away from Cosmos 2542, which in turn tweaked its own orbit to get closer again. "This is all circumstantial evidence," the watcher wrote, but "a hell of a lot of circumstances make it look like a known Russian inspection satellite is currently inspecting a known U.S. spy satellite."

Laura Grego, an astrophysicist who studies space technology, saw the tweets; she catalogues satellites, so she has been reading amateur watchers' communications, she says, "since before Twitter was invented." One country's satellite stalking another's is exactly what people like Grego, who worry about space war, worry about. Space war is not warfighters shooting one another in space. Nor is it war from the highest of all military high grounds: "Satellites don't 'drop' bombs," Grego says, "and aren't faster, better or less expensive than other ways of bombing." Space war is war on satellites. Cosmos 2542 could have been equipped to interfere with or damage USA 245 or to blow it to pieces. And if it had done so, the U.S. might have retaliated, perhaps by destroying a Russian spacecraft, and we might have had a space war. And then which satellites, and which services civilization depends on, would be destroyed?

For the U.S. more than anyone else, space war could be ruinous. The country relies heavily on its satellites to transmit signals for GPS, credit-card transactions, hospital systems, television stations, weather reports; the list goes on and on. But it depends more than any other country on its military satellites for communication and surveillance. And all satellites–bright and moving in predictable, public orbits–are essentially sitting ducks, nearly impossible to defend; space war is what the military calls "offense-dominant."

The U.S. military's solution to vulnerability is, of course, military. Last December the Department of Defense created the Space Force, saying that Russia and China had "weaponized space" and that space is now a "warfighting domain." Space Force's job is to protect U.S. satellites and to respond to bad behavior by adversaries.

Cosmos 2542, as the then head of Space Force, General John Raymond, sternly told Time magazine, "has the potential to create a dangerous situation in space." But Cosmos 2542's stalking turned out not to start a space war. Neither Grego nor the amateur watchers know what Cosmos was doing, but their best guess is that it was something like what Russian trawlers do when they hang around U.S. Navy ships: annoy, or intimidate if possible, and see what they can see. In any case, in mid-March the amateur watcher tweeted that USA 245 had made a small maneuver "that will put it at a distance of thousands of kilometers for weeks to come if not months," and after that Cosmos 2542 took itself elsewhere. Before it did, Grego added her own tweet: "A good time to establish some shared understandings about how close is too close."

Grego is at the Union of Concerned Scientists, a nonprofit that is part of the three worlds–nongovernmental organization (NGO), military and diplomatic–focused on space war. To her, the best way to stop a space war is to enter an international agreement to prevent or limit one. So far negotiations are stalled in international politics. Diplomats never work fast, Grego says, but right now they are "splashing around in the puddle of diplomacy" without getting much done.

So here we are, with the possibility of an escalating space war that would bring certain and incalculable civilian consequences. Yet attempts at diplomacy have been lackluster, and the military's response sounds as aggressive as it does protective. "I don't know if space war is imminent," says John Lauder, a 30-year veteran of the intelligence community's arms-control monitoring efforts, "but there are trends that make space more dangerous. It's not sitting on top of us, but it's moving in our direction at a rapid speed."

Space Pearl Harbor

For almost as long as there have been satellites, there have been weapons to use against them and networks to track them. Satellite number one, of course, was Sputnik 1, put into orbit by the former U.S.S.R. on October 4, 1957. Sputnik and its successors were tracked immediately by amateurs with cameras; by February 1959 the Defense Advanced Research Projects Agency had set up the first satellite-surveillance network. The first antisatellite weapon was a missile called High Virgo, launched by the U.S. on September 22, 1959. In 1963 the former U.S.S.R. tested the first "satellite fighter"; in a 1968 test, another satellite fighter entered the same orbit as a U.S.S.R. target satellite, maneuvered next to it and exploded.

After this energized beginning, the U.S. and the former Soviet Union turned their attention from space war to the nuclear balances of the cold war. The U.S. spent the subsequent decades building satellites that were "exquisitely capable and costing billions of dollars and functioning very, very well," says Brian Weeden of the Secure World Foundation. "But they were not built with the idea of having an adversary do something to them." Once the U.S.S.R. collapsed, he says, "America thought it would be dominant in space forever."

Space war appeared briefly on the U.S. agenda in 2001, when a security commission report, headed by Donald Rumsfeld before he left to become secretary of defense, warned of U.S. vulnerability and included the notable phrase "a Space Pearl Harbor." Douglas Loverro, then an air force program director, began advocating for a kind of space force, but "9/11 happened, and everybody forgot about space," he says.

Meanwhile, Grego says, France, Japan, the U.K. and India had launched their own satellites, and more nations had built, bought or operated satellites launched by others. Loverro and other officials, helped by Representatives Mike Rogers of Alabama and Jim Cooper of Tennessee, both on the House Armed Services Committee, kept pushing for a space branch of the military and got nowhere until December 2019, when Space Force was created by presidential fiat. "Magically, we were revived," Loverro says.

This suddenness meant that for a while, Space Force was long on rhetoric but short on specifics and subject to snide remarks from people on the Internet. Its public image was not helped when its first official act was to design uniforms (camouflage, even for soldiers whose field of battle is in front of a computer) and a logo (the delta-shaped wing shared by patches of the U.S. Air Force and the National Reconnaissance Office–and *Star Trek*). By June, however, Space Force and its Combatant Command, U.S. Space Command, were recruiting tech-smart people; coordinating with international allies; deciding which technologies to buy; and running war-game simulations in which teams attack, counterattack and outthink one another. Space war "doesn't have to be inevitable," says Brigadier General Thomas James, commander at Joint Task Force–Space Defense, a component of Space Command, but "it's very serious business, and we take it seriously."

Offense and Defense

Anyone attacking satellites can choose from a long, varied menu of weapons. The splashiest option, called a direct-ascent antisatellite weapon, or DA-ASAT, is a missile shot from Earth that blows up a spacecraft. The U.S. and Russia have had DA-ASAT missiles since the cold war. China and India have both tested DA-ASATs on their own satellites. Russia's latest test was this past April.

Another option for attacking satellites is a maneuverable satellite, like Cosmos 2542, which can approach another country's vehicle. Satellites have often used small engines to move for safety reasons, such as to avoid space debris, and maneuverable satellites could be used for refueling or repair. But maneuverable satellites can be dual use, equally capable of colliding with other satellites or of spying on or shooting them. In the past few years the U.S. and

Russia have used satellites to deploy smaller subsatellites that roam around: Cosmos 2542 emitted Cosmos 2543, which also stalked USA 245. The U.S. has the X-37B, a smaller, robotic version of the Space Shuttle that does generally secret things, including emitting subsatellites. What these subsatellites can do that parent satellites cannot is also secret and therefore unclear: Weeden says that all we know about them is what we see.

A space war technology that we cannot see, in contrast, is electromagnetic radiation. Satellites can carry equipment to jam others' communications from or to ground stations, or they can mount spoofing attacks to trick other satellites into communicating the wrong things. The U.S., China and Russia routinely jam other countries' links with navigation satellites. Lasers on satellites or on the ground can dazzle or blind spy satellites' imaging sensors, although exactly who has what laser technology with which capabilities is, again, classified or unknown.

In all these hostilities, the U.S. has much to lose. Of the 3,200 or so functioning satellites, the U.S. owns 1,327. Of those, 935 are commercial satellites that provide broadcasting and secure, global communications. Around 200 U.S. satellites are government and scientific satellites that collect data for predicting hurricanes, monitoring droughts, watching the creep of continents and, like the Hubble Space Telescope, understanding the universe. The remaining handful are military and intelligence satellites, most of which are used for communications–command and control of forces, for example, or directing of drones–and for spying. Together the satellites enable modern civilization. They provide the Internet access and GPS navigation and timing signals on which everyone in the world depends and support industries from banking to food supply, the power grid, transportation, the news media and health care.

The few military and intelligence satellites are fundamental to U.S. security and are the source of its vulnerability. The early-missile-warning system uses only 10 satellites, the intelligence community's high-resolution imagery is provided by maybe a dozen, and military command and control communications depend on just six. "The central military problem has been," Grego says, "that we extended ourselves into space, and now we're vulnerable."

This vulnerability matters because no one is sure how satellites can be defended. Perhaps imaging satellites could be fitted with a shutter that reacts fast to too much light, or bodyguard satellites could protect other satellites. Whether such defenses have been put into practice is unknown. "You won't find a lot of official details on the technologies for defense," Weeden says, "due to classification." "Cloaking" a satellite is technically possible, he says, but also expensive and difficult. You can make a spacecraft dark to radar or to telescopes but not to both, and the process can hamper the satellite's performance.

Most efforts at defense tend to focus on deterrence. "The natural place for the military to go is deterrence by punishment," Grego says. "You use ASAT on me; I'll use it on you." The first problem with punishment, though, is unpredictable escalation. The second is the flip side of U.S. vulnerability–that Russia and China do not need their military satellites as much as the U.S. does. "It's only really the U.S. that needs to conduct military operations anywhere in the world all the time against anyone," Weeden says, whereas most of Russia's and China's need for defense communications is local or regional and "can generally be solved with [other] means."

Alternatively the U.S. could deter attacks by denying their benefits. In other words, a redundant, resilient system that could take losses without losing effectiveness would not be as attractive a target. This is standard deterrence theory; whether the Pentagon is practicing it is not clear. The official Defense Space Strategy, published this past June, avoided this level of detail in the unclassified version of the report.

Deterrence by denial of benefits is effectively being supplied, however, by the commercial space industry. Traditionally the Pentagon has contracted with defense-industry giants such as Lockheed Martin, Raytheon and Northrop Grumman to build its satellites. These spacecraft tend to be the size of large pickup trucks, and one reason for that is economic efficiency, says Colonel Eric Felt of the Air Force Research Laboratory's Space Vehicles Directorate. Whatever new function you need, he says, "just glue it on to whatever you're building." The so-called New Space companies, however—SpaceX, Blue Origin, Virgin Galactic, Planet—have reusable launchers and satellites the size of watermelons at a quarter to a tenth the cost. The savings allow the military to launch more satellites more often, Felt says, spreading out different functions to different vehicles and making replacement easier.

New Space companies are linking hundreds or thousands of small satellites into large constellations that ensure Internet access and continuous imaging coverage of every spot on the globe and serve as textbook denial of benefits. The Space-Based Infrared System (SBIRS), in contrast, is a constellation of 10 large early-warning satellites and is "a fat, juicy target," says Joshua Huminski, director of the National Security Space Program at the Center for the Study of the Presidency and Congress.* "I hit three SBIRS satellites, and you don't have early warning." But if SBIRS were a megaconstellation of small satellites, he says, "I take out three, and it's annoying, but the constellation will heal itself."

Felt says that Space Force is developing close relationships with New Space companies, is adopting New Space's rule for ordering new technology not by specification but by function ("I need a five-inch coffee mug" versus "I need a caffeine-delivery system") and is buying good-enough commercial imagery with a credit card.

Space Diplomacy

By mid-July, months after Cosmos 2542 emitted Cosmos 2543 and drifted away from USA 245, amateur trackers noticed that Cosmos 2543 was suddenly accompanied by a projectile, Object 45915, which then zoomed off, apparently using its own motor, at more than 700 kilometers per hour. Raymond called it an "on-orbit weapons test." The U.K.'s Ministry of Defense tweeted that it hoped Russia would work with international partners toward responsible behavior in space.

Getting spacefaring countries to agree to behave themselves is not simple. International law governing space is a work in progress: NGOs are working on space-law manuals, Weeden says, but "law about conflict in space is so far undefined." International binding treaties are nonspecific or old or on indefinite hold. The United Nations Charter prohibits threats to territorial integrity that extend to outer space. The Outer Space Treaty bans nuclear weapons in space but was signed in 1967, before the great advances in space technologies. In 2014 Russia and China proposed the Prevention of the Placement of Weapons in Outer Space treaty, which prohibits stationing weapons in space; the U.S. does not agree to the proposal's terms but has made no counterproposal. Most recently, the U.N. Committee on the Peaceful Uses of Outer Space agreed on 21 nonbinding guidelines for behavior–for example, "adopt, revise and amend, as necessary, national regulatory frameworks for outer space activities"–which, Grego says, took "a considerable amount of work but do seem a little vague and underwhelming when you read them. You would be disappointed if you hoped they would address space war, but they are not meant to."

The issues on which countries would have to agree are complex and prickly. How do you include everyone–not just the elephantine U.S.-China-Russia triad but all 10 or so countries that can reach space? What is the definition of "weapons" when, say, a robot arm could be used either to replace a defunct sensor or to grab another country's satellite? How to set up lines of communication so that a message of "Sorry, I didn't mean to hit your satellite" can go out before miscalculation and escalation occur? What counts as aggression–hitting another country's satellite with a DA-ASAT missile? Sidling up to another country's satellite? How close is too close? How do you verify that no one cheats on an agreement? And which targets for attacks would cross the line into war, asks John Klein, a fellow at Falcon Research and an instructor at George Washington University's Space Policy Institute? "If you blow up all the GPS satellites–that's critical infrastructure; that's probably war. Take out a small satellite, probably not war."

Meanwhile, Grego points out, countries more or less abide by unofficial norms of behavior: registering new satellites sent into orbit, deorbiting their dying ones to avoid creating debris, not testing DA-ASATs on their own satellites and not destroying another country's satellites. So if a binding treaty is too hard, how about a nonbinding international agreement based on current norms? "The U.S. and Russia are talking about this," Lauder says. "Not that we know in detail what they're talking about, but that they're talking is a good thing. Because nobody can be confident of winning a space war."

Grego agrees with the consensus that it is best to use current norms as a starting point in talks, but she is a little fed up with the pace of diplomacy's progress. The situation "should have been managed years ago by some kind of agreed limits," she says. Shouldn't the State Department get going on this? "We are," says Eric Desautels, director of the Office of Emerging Security Challenges at the State Department. In July 2020 U.S. and Russian officials discussed opening lines of communication to prevent miscalculation and escalation–the first such discussion since 2013–and expressed interest in continuing the discussion. Meanwhile the U.S. supports a new U.N. agreement that would "break the impasse" on space and also reduce risk of escalation.

Always Watching

The fundamental necessity of space security is knowing where every satellite is and how it is behaving. Space Force's June 2020 doctrine calls this "space domain awareness." Officially that awareness comes via a global network of sensors on satellites and telescopes on the ground that covers all orbits all the time and tracks everything bigger than 10 centimeters: 3,200 live satellites, as well as 24,000 nonfunctioning "zombies" and pieces of space debris that, in a collision with a satellite at 35,400 kilometers an hour, would cause a catastrophic breakup.

The information is sent to Space Force's 18th Space Control Squadron at the Combined Space Operations Center at Vandenberg Air Force Base in California. Data on the secret satellites are set aside, and the rest go into a public, free, online catalog called Space-Track, from which "conjunction notifications" are issued when two satellites look like they might get too close.

The 18th Space Control Squadron works in a secretive operations center that, judging by press release photographs, values functionality over hominess–a maze of connected computer desks, banks of wall monitors and shiny metal letters spelling out "Where Space Superiority Begins" on a beige wall. In this barn of a room, five to seven members of the 18th Squadron sit next to one another and, to ensure complete and accurate analyses, also next to their colleagues from the U.K., Australia, Canada, NASA and the Department of Commerce, as well as a representative from a collective of New Space companies (all with security clearances). Not on the same floor but available nearby for consultation are representatives from France, Germany and the U.S. intelligence community, including the National Reconnaissance Office. Most people in the 18th Squadron are younger than 25 years, although some experienced "graybeards" bring the average age up to 27. All are tech whizzes. "They've blown my socks off," says Lieutenant Colonel Justin Sorice, the 18th's commander.

The 18th Squadron can say only so much about the details of its job. To find out how to track a satellite, ask the amateurs. They prefer to be called hobbyists; 20 to 100 of them are active, lots are retirees and all are tech-minded. They use binoculars and stopwatches or radio receivers–although sometimes they get fancier–and provide global coverage by being international. They sometimes communicate on Twitter but mostly use a public mailing list called SeeSat, which is how Grego followed them pre-Twitter. "I stopped calling them amateurs a long time ago," she says. "They're quite skilled."

Their low-tech approach means they track mainly the brightest, biggest satellites. They pick spacecraft from Space-Track, from Web sites listing which satellites will be over which cities on a given night, or from rocket-launch notices telling navigators to avoid particular areas. They watch the satellite pass a star, and they hit a timer. As they watch it pass a second star, they check the time to a fraction of a second. By knowing the stars' positions and the time, they can derive an orbit. The last time the secret X-37B, a maneuverable satellite/spy plane, flew, the hobbyists had its orbit in 24 hours.

"The orbit gives a surprising amount of information," says Jonathan C. McDowell, a hobbyist and an astronomer at the Center for Astrophysics | Harvard & Smithsonian. Many satellites, for instance, are in low Earth orbit (LEO), which is up to 2,000 kilometers high. These see the least area but take the crispest pictures, so satellites in LEO are often imagers either doing science, such as monitoring weather, or spying. Others in geosynchronous orbit (GEO), at 35,786 kilometers, hover over and move exactly with one spot on Earth. "You've effectively built a 35,000-kilometer tower," McDowell says, "and taken away the tower," so the satellites in GEO are mostly for communications or broadcasting. Satellites in highly elliptical orbits usually spend most of their time over the Northern Hemisphere and tend to be early-warning or spy satellites. And in sun-synchronous orbits, satellites keep in lockstep with the sun so that the shadows on Earth are unchanging–perfect for spying.

Information also comes from a satellite's behavior. If it is adjusting its orbit, it could be countering Earth's drag or watching one spot on Earth: "During the 1973 war," McDowell says, referring to the Yom Kippur War between Israel and a coalition of Arab states, "satellites moved to give more frequent passes over Egypt." Satellites can "flare" when the sun glints off their flat surfaces; if the flaring is random, the satellite is tumbling out of orbit.

McDowell thinks maybe 10 percent of the satellites they track are classified– spacecraft for military command and control, early-warning equipment, and radio and optical spy satellites–some of which are high-resolution instruments that resemble the Hubble Space Telescope but look down instead of up. These do not show up on Space-Track. The hobbyists are the only open source of information on all countries' classified satellites and, Weeden says, a "primary source of data on American military objects." These space watchers are aware that they bear a responsibility to be careful of speculating about how a spy satellite is being used, McDowell says, but on the whole they are not worried about revealing national secrets: rival countries can buy binoculars and stopwatches, too.

In any case, McDowell thinks the hobbyists are generally apolitical. The enemy, as they see it, is not as another country but the failures of function to which machines are prone, such as RUD (rapid unplanned disassembly), and IOBM (in oceans by mistake). They see themselves, as the 18th Squadron surely must, "as an international community of engineers in space battling Murphy's Law and nature," McDowell says. And they like solving puzzles, finding the gaps in Space-Track left for classified satellites and filling them in: "It's the Sudoku thing," McDowell says.

Ultimately the hobbyists matter in the way that oversight and transparency always matter. Everything about satellites and space war is beset with secrecy–some necessary, some perhaps not. If the hobbyists had not published the Cosmos stalking, Grego says, the U.S. would have been free not to acknowledge a vulnerability, and Russia would have been free to deny that anything had happened. These hobbyists, she says, "can be powerful in their own way." The military and the diplomats work secretly in their own spheres, but if the rest of us want to track the probability of space war, the hobbyists are out there making sure it is as open source as possible.

**Editor's Note (11/20/20): This sentence has been revised after posting to clarify Joshua Huminski's primary affiliation.*

About the Author

Ann Finkbeiner is a science writer based in Baltimore. She specializes in writing about astronomy and cosmology, grief, and the intersection of science and national security. She is co-proprietor of the science blog The Last Word on Nothing.

Space Wars - Coming to the Sky Near You?

By Theresa Hitchens

Take the high ground and hold it!" has been standard combat doctrine for armies since ancient times. Now that people and their machines have entered outer space, it is no surprise that generals the world over regard Earth orbit as the key to modern warfare. But until recently, a norm had developed against the weaponization of space–even though there are no international treaties or laws explicitly prohibiting nonnuclear antisatellite systems or weapons placed in orbit. Nations mostly shunned such weapons, fearing the possibility of destabilizing the global balance of power with a costly arms race in space.

> *In war, do not launch an ascending attack head-on against the enemy who holds the high ground. Do not engage the enemy when he makes a descending attack from high ground. Lure him to level ground to do battle.*
>
> *–Sun Tzu, Chinese military strategist,*
> *The Art of War, circa 500 B.C.*

That consensus is now in danger of unraveling. In October 2006 the Bush administration adopted a new, rather vaguely worded National Space Policy that asserts the right of the U.S. to conduct "space control" and rejects "new legal regimes or other restrictions that seek to prohibit or limit U.S. access to or use of space." Three months later the People's Republic of China shocked the world by shooting down one of its own aging Fengyun weather satellites, an act that resulted in a hailstorm of dangerous orbital debris and a deluge of international protests, not to mention a good deal of hand-wringing in American military and political circles. The launch was the first test of a dedicated antisatellite weapon in more than two decades–making China only the third country, after the U.S. and the Russian Federation, to have demonstrated such a technology. Many observers wondered whether the test might be the first shot in an emerging era of space warfare.

Critics maintain it is not at all clear that a nation's security would be enhanced by developing the means to wage space war. After all, satellites and even orbiting weapons, by their very nature, are relatively easy to spot and easy to track, and they are likely to remain highly vulnerable to attack no matter what defense measures are taken. Further, developing antisatellite systems would almost surely lead to a hugely expensive and potentially runaway arms race, as other countries would conclude that they, too, must compete. And even tests of the technology needed to conduct space battles—not to mention a real battle—could generate enormous amounts of wreckage that would continue to orbit Earth. Converging on satellites and crewed space vehicles at speeds approaching several miles a second, such space debris would threaten satellite-based telecommunications, weather forecasting, precision navigation, even military command and control, potentially sending the world's economy back to the 1950s.

"Star Wars" Redux

Since the dawn of the space age, defense planners have hatched concepts for antisatellite and space-based weaponry—all in the interest of exploiting the military advantages of the ultimate high ground. Perhaps the most notable effort was President Ronald Reagan's Strategic Defense Initiative (SDI)—derided by its critics as "Star Wars." Yet by and large, U.S. military strategy has never embraced such weapons.

Traditionally, space weapons have been defined as destructive systems that operate in outer space after having been launched directly from Earth or parked in orbit. The category includes antisatellite weapons; laser systems that couple ground-based lasers with airship- or satellite-mounted mirrors, which could reflect a laser beam beyond the ground horizon; and orbital platforms that could fire projectiles or energy beams from space. (It is important to note that all nations would presumably avoid using a fourth kind of antisatellite weapon, namely, a high-altitude nuclear explosion. The electromagnetic pulse and cloud of highly charged particles created by such a blast would likely disable or destroy nearly all satellites and manned spacecraft in orbit [see "Nuclear Explosions in Orbit," by Daniel G. Dupont; *Scientific American*, June 2004].)

But virtually no statement about space weapons goes politically uncontested. Recently some proponents of such weapons have sought to expand the long-held classification I just described to include two existing technologies that depend on passage through space: intercontinental ballistic missiles (ICBMs) and ground-based electronic warfare systems. Their existence, or so the argument goes, renders moot any question about whether to build space weapons systems. By the revised definition, after all, "space weapons" already exist. Whatever the exact meaning of the term, however, the questions such weapons raise are hardly new to think tanks and military-planning circles in Washington: Is it desirable, or even feasible, to incorporate antisatellite weapons and weapons fired from orbit into the nation's military strategy?

The new National Space Policy, coupled with the Chinese test, has brought renewed urgency to that behind-the-scenes debate. Many American military leaders expressed alarm in the wake of the Chinese test, worrying that in any conflict over Taiwan, China could threaten U.S. satellites in low Earth orbit. In April 2007 Michael Moseley, the U.S. Air Force chief of staff, compared China's antisatellite test with the launch of Sputnik by the Soviet Union in 1957, an act that singularly intensified the arms race during the cold war. Moseley also revealed that the Pentagon had begun reviewing the nation's satellite defenses, explaining that outer space was now a "contested domain."

Congressional reaction fell along predictable political lines. Conservative "China hawks" such as Senator Jon Kyl of Arizona immediately called for the development of antisatellite weapons and space-based interceptors to counter Chinese capabilities.

Meanwhile more moderate politicians, including Representative Edward Markey of Massachusetts, urged the Bush administration to begin negotiations aimed at banning all space weapons.

International Power Plays

Perhaps of even greater concern is that several other nations, including one of China's regional rivals, India, may feel compelled to seek offensive as well as defensive capabilities in space. The U.S. trade journal Defense News, for instance, quoted unidentified Indian defense officials as stating that their country had already begun developing its own kinetic-energy (nonexplosive, hit-to-kill) and laser-based antisatellite weapons.

If India goes down that path, its archrival Pakistan will probably follow suit. Like India, Pakistan has a well-developed ballistic missile program, including medium-range missiles that could launch an antisatellite system. Even Japan, the third major Asian power, might join such a space race. In June 2007 the National Diet of Japan began considering a bill backed by the current Fukuda government that would permit the development of satellites for "military and national security" purposes.

As for Russia, in the wake of the Chinese test President Vladimir Putin reiterated Moscow's stance against the weaponization of space. At the same time, though, he refused to criticize Beijing's actions and blamed the U.S. instead. The American efforts to build a missile defense system, Putin charged, and the increasingly aggressive American plans for a military position in space were prompting China's moves. Yet Russia itself, as a major spacefaring power that has incorporated satellites into its national security structure, would be hard-pressed to forgo entering an arms race in space.

Given the proliferation of spacefaring entities, proponents of a robust space warfare strategy believe that arming the heavens is inevitable and that it would be best for the U.S. to get there first with firepower. Antisatellite and space-based weapons, they argue, will be necessary not only to defend U.S. military and commercial satellites but also to deny any future adversary the use of space capabilities to enhance the performance of its forces on the battlefield.

Yet any arms race in space would almost inevitably destabilize the balance of power and thereby multiply the risks of global conflict. In such headlong competition–whether in space or elsewhere–equilibrium among the adversaries would be virtually impossible to maintain. Even if the major powers did achieve stability, that reality would still provide no guarantee that both sides would perceive it to be so. The moment one side saw itself to be slipping behind the other, the first side would be strongly tempted to launch a preemptive strike, before things got even worse. Ironically, the same would hold for the side that perceived itself to have gained an advantage. Again, there would be strong temptation to strike first, before the adversary could catch up. Finally, a space weapons race would ratchet up the chances that a mere technological mistake could trigger a battle. After all, in the distant void, reliably distinguishing an intentional act from an accidental one would be highly problematic.

Hit-to-Kill Interceptors

According to assessments by U.S. military and intelligence officials as well as by independent experts, the Chinese probably destroyed their weather satellite with a kinetic-energy vehicle boosted by a two-stage medium-range ballistic missile. Technologically, launching such direct-ascent antisatellite weapons is one of the simplest ways to take out a satellite. About a dozen nations and consortia can reach low Earth orbit (between roughly 100 and 2,000 kilometers, or 60 to 1,250 miles, high) with a medium-range missile; eight of those countries can reach geostationary orbit (about 36,000 kilometers, or 22,000 miles, above Earth).

But the real technical hurdle to making a hit-to-kill vehicle is not launch capacity; it is the precision maneuverability and guidance technology needed to steer the vehicle into its target. Just how well China has mastered those techniques is unclear. Because the weather satellite was still operating when it was destroyed, the Chinese operators would have known its exact location at all times.

Ground-Based Lasers

The test of China's direct-ascent antisatellite device came on the heels of press reports in September 2006 that the Chinese had also managed to "paint," or illuminate, U.S. spy satellites with a ground-based laser. Was Beijing actually trying to "blind" or otherwise damage the satellites? No one knows, and no consensus seems to have emerged in official Washington circles about the Chinese intent. Perhaps China was simply testing how well its network of low-power laser-ranging stations could track American orbital observation platforms.

Even so, the test was provocative. Not all satellites have to be electronically "fried" to be put out of commission. A 1997 test of the army's MIRACL system (for midinfrared advanced chemical laser) showed that satellites designed to collect optical images can be temporarily disrupted–dazzled–by low-power beams. It follows that among the satellites vulnerable to such an attack are the orbital spies.

The U.S. and the former Soviet Union began experimenting with laser-based antisatellite weapons in the 1970s. Engineers in both countries have focused on the many problems of building high-power laser systems that could reliably destroy low-flying satellites from the ground. Such systems could be guided by "adaptive optics": deformable mirrors that can continuously compensate for atmospheric distortions. But tremendous amounts of energy would be needed to feed high-power lasers, and even then the range and effectiveness of the beams would be severely limited by dispersion, by attenuation as they passed through smoke or clouds, and by the difficulty of keeping the beams on-target long enough to do damage.

During the development of the SDI, the U.S. conducted several laser experiments from Hawaii, including a test in which a beam was bounced off a mirror mounted on a satellite. Laser experiments continue at the Starfire Optical Range at Kirtland Air Force Base in New Mexico. Pentagon budget documents from fiscal years 2004 through 2007 listed antisatellite operations among the goals of the Starfire research, but that language was removed from budget documents in fiscal year 2008 after Congress made inquiries. The Starfire system incorporates adaptive optics that narrow the outgoing laser beam and thus increase the density of its power. That capability is not required for imagery or tracking, further suggesting that Starfire could be used as a weapon.

Yet despite decades of work, battle-ready versions of directed-energy weapons still seem far away. An air force planning document, for instance, predicted in 2003 that a ground-based weapon able to "propagate laser beams through the atmosphere to [stun or kill low Earth orbit] satellites" could be available between 2015 and 2030. Given the current state of research, even those dates seem optimistic.

Co-orbital Satellites

Recent advances in miniaturized sensors, powerful onboard computers and efficient rocket thrusters have made a third kind of antisatellite technology increasingly feasible: the offensive microsatellite. One example that demonstrates the potential is the air force's experimental satellite series (XSS) project, which is developing microsatellites intended to conduct "autonomous proximity operations" around larger satellites. The first two microsatellites in the program, the XSS-10 and XSS-11, were launched in 2003 and 2005. Though ostensibly intended to inspect larger satellites, such microsatellites could also ram target satellites or carry explosives or directed-energy payloads such as radio-frequency jamming systems or high-powered microwave emitters. Air force budget documents show that the XSS effort is tied to a program called Advanced Weapons Technology, which is dedicated to research on military laser and microwave systems.

During the cold war the Soviet Union developed, tested and even declared operational a co-orbital antisatellite system–a maneuverable interceptor with an explosive payload that was launched by missile into an orbit near a target satellite in low Earth orbit. In effect, the device was a smart "space mine," but it was last demonstrated in 1982 and is probably no longer working. Today such an interceptor would likely be a microsatellite that could be parked in an orbit that would cross the orbits of several of its potential targets. It could then be activated on command during a close encounter.

In 2005 the air force described a program that would provide "localized" space "situational awareness" and "anomaly characterization" for friendly host satellites in geostationary orbit. The program is dubbed ANGELS (for autonomous nanosatellite guardian for evaluating local space), and the budget line believed to represent it focuses on acquiring "high value space asset defensive capabilities," including a "warning sensor for detection of a direct ascent or co-orbital vehicle." It is clear that such guardian nanosatellites could also serve as offensive weapons if they were maneuvered close to enemy satellites.

And the list goes on. A "parasitic satellite" would shadow or even attach itself to a target in geostationary orbit. Farsat, which was mentioned in an appendix to the [Donald] Rumsfeld Space Commission report in 2001, "would be placed in a 'storage' orbit (perhaps with many microsatellites housed inside) relatively far from its target but ready to be maneuvered in for a kill."

Finally, the air force proposed some time ago a space-based radio-frequency weapon system, which "would be a constellation of satellites containing high-power radio-frequency transmitters that possess the capability to disrupt/destroy/disable a wide variety of electronics and national-level command and control systems."

Air force planning documents from 2003 envisioned that such a technology would emerge after 2015. But outside experts think that orbital radio-frequency and microwave weapons are technically feasible today and could be deployed in the relatively near future.

Space Bombers

Though not by definition a space weapon, the Pentagon's Common Aero Vehicle/Hypersonic Technology Vehicle (often called CAV) enters into this discussion because, like an ICBM, it would travel through space to strike Earth-bound targets. An unpowered but highly maneuverable hypersonic glide vehicle, the CAV would be deployed from a future hypersonic space plane, swoop down into the atmosphere from orbit and drop conventional bombs on ground targets. Congress recently began funding the project but, to avoid stoking a potential arms race in space, has prohibited any work to place weapons on the CAV. Although engineers are making steady progress on the key technologies for the CAV program, both the vehicle and its space plane mothership are still likely decades off.

Some of the congressional sensitivity to the design of the CAV may have arisen from another, much more controversial space weapons concept with parallel goals: hypervelocity rod bundles that would be dropped to Earth from orbital platforms. For decades air force planners have been thinking about placing weapons in orbit that could strike terrestrial targets, particularly buried, "hardened" bunkers and caches of weapons of mass destruction. Commonly called "rods from God," the bundles would be made up of large tungsten rods, each as long as six meters (20 feet) and 30 centimeters (12 inches) across. Each rod would be hurled downward from an orbiting spacecraft and guided to its target at tremendous speed.

Both high costs and the laws of physics, however, challenge their feasibility. Ensuring that the projectiles do not burn up or deform from reentry friction while sustaining a precise, nearly vertical flight path would be extremely difficult. Calculations indicate that the nonexplosive rods would probably be no more effective than more conventional munitions. Furthermore, the expense of lofting the heavy projectiles into orbit would be exorbitant. Thus, despite continued interest in them, rods from God seem to fall into the realm of science fiction.

Obstacles to Space Weapons

What, then, is holding the U.S. (and other nations) back from a full-bore pursuit of space weapons? The countervailing pressures are threefold: political opposition, technological challenges and high costs.

The American body politic is deeply divided over the wisdom of making space warfare a part of the national military strategy. The risks are manifold. I remarked earlier on the general instabilities of an arms race, but there is a further issue of stability among the nuclear powers. Early-warning and spy satellites have traditionally played a crucial role in reducing fears of a surprise nuclear attack. But if antisatellite weapons disabled those eyes-in-the-sky, the resulting uncertainty and distrust could rapidly lead to catastrophe.

One of the most serious technological challenges posed by space weapons is the proliferation of space debris, to which I alluded earlier. According to investigators at the air force, NASA and Celestrak (an independent space-monitoring Web site), the Chinese antisatellite test left more than 2,000 pieces of junk, baseball-size and larger, orbiting the globe in a cloud that lies between about 200 kilometers (125 miles) and 4,000 kilometers (2,500 miles) above Earth's surface. Perhaps another 150,000 objects that are a centimeter (half an inch) across and larger were released. High orbital velocities make even tiny pieces of space junk dangerous to spacecraft of all kinds. And ground stations cannot reliably monitor or track objects smaller than about five centimeters (two inches) across in low Earth orbit (around a meter in geostationary orbit), a capability that might enable satellites to maneuver out of the way. To avoid being damaged by the Chinese space debris, in fact, two U.S. satellites had to alter course. Any shooting war in space would raise the specter of a polluted space environment no longer navigable by Earth-orbiting satellites.

Basing weapons in orbit also presents difficult technical obstacles. They would be just as vulnerable as satellites are to all kinds of outside agents: space debris, projectiles, electromagnetic signals, even natural micrometeoroids. Shielding space weapons against such threats would also be impractical, mostly because shielding is bulky and adds mass, thereby greatly increasing launch costs. Orbital weapons would be mostly autonomous mechanisms, which would make operational errors and failures likely. The paths of objects in orbit are relatively easy to predict, which would make hiding large weapons problematic. And because satellites in low Earth orbit are overhead for only a few minutes at a time, keeping one of them constantly in range would require many weapons.

Finally, getting into space and operating there is extremely expensive: between $2,000 and $10,000 a pound to reach low Earth orbit and between $15,000 and $20,000 a pound for geostationary orbit. Each space-based weapon would require replacement every seven to 15 years, and in-orbit repairs would not be cheap, either.

Alternatives to Space Warfare

Given the risks of space warfare to national and international security, as well as the technical and financial hurdles that must be overcome, it would seem only prudent for spacefaring nations to find ways to prevent an arms race in space. The U.S. focus has been to reduce the vulnerability of its satellite fleet and explore alternatives to its dependence on satellite services. Most other space-capable countries are instead seeking multilateral diplomatic and legal measures. The options range from treaties that would ban antisatellite and space-based weapons to voluntary measures that would help build transparency and mutual confidence.

The Bush administration has adamantly opposed any form of negotiations regarding space weapons. Opponents of multilateral space weapons agreements contend that others (particularly China) will sign up but build secret arsenals at the same time, because such treaty violations cannot be detected. They argue further that the U.S. cannot sit idly as potential adversaries gain spaceborne resources that could enhance their terrestrial combat capabilities.

Proponents of international treaties counter that failure to negotiate such agreements entails real opportunity costs. An arms race in space may end up compromising the security of all nations, including that of the U.S., while it stretches the economic capacities of the competitors to the breaking point. And whereas many advocates of a space weapons ban concede that it will be difficult to construct a fully verifiable treaty—because space technology can be used for both military and civilian ends—effective treaties already exist that do not require strict verification. A good example is the Biological Weapons Convention. Certainly a prohibition on the testing and use (as opposed to the deployment) of the most dangerous class of near-term space weapons—destructive (as opposed to jamming) antisatellite systems—would be easily verifiable, because earthbound observers can readily detect orbital debris. Furthermore, any party to a treaty would know that all its space launches would be tracked from the ground, and any suspicious object in orbit would promptly be labeled as such. The international outcry that would ensue from such overt treaty violations could deter would-be violators.

Since the mid-1990s, however, progress on establishing a new multilateral space regime has lagged. The U.S. has blocked efforts at the United Nations Conference on Disarmament in Geneva to begin negotiations on a treaty to ban space weapons. China, meanwhile, has refused to accept anything less. Hence, intermediate measures such as voluntary confidence-building, space traffic control or a code of responsible conduct for spacefaring nations have remained stalled.

Space warfare is not inevitable. But the recent policy shift in the U.S. and China's provocative actions have highlighted the fact that the world is approaching a crossroads. Countries must come to grips with their strong self-interest in preventing the testing and use of orbital weapons. The nations of Earth must soon decide whether it is possible to sustain the predominantly peaceful human space exploration that has already lasted half a century. The likely alternative would be unacceptable to all.

About the Author

Theresa Hitchens directs the Center for Defense Information in Washington, D.C., and leads its Space Security Project, in cooperation with the Secure World Foundation. She is author of Future Security in Space: Charting a Cooperative Course *(2004) and was editor of* Defense News *from 1998 until 2000. As a journalist, she has focused on the military, the defense industry and North Atlantic Treaty Organization affairs. Most recently, Hitchens served as director of research at the British American Security Information Council, a defense think tank.*

Enhanced Armor

By Steven Ashley

It's an all-too-familiar scene from the war in Iraq: A video shows a convoy of combat vehicles patrolling a dusty causeway. Suddenly, a huge detonation erupts next to one, often followed by a determined ambush. Over time, the guerrillas have steadily upgraded the lethality of their roadside bombs, suicide assaults and surprise attacks. This year, however, the U.S. military plans to field several new armor systems that should better defend its vehicles and personnel.

"The need to stop multiple, ever evolving threats is a tough problem," states Tony Russell, chief technology officer at Armor Holdings, a security products maker based in Jacksonville, Fla. "The systems we develop must defeat repeated armor-piercing bullet hits as well as the fragments and blast overpressures from explosives. And no one material–metal, composite, ceramic–is best at stopping every threat." Moreover, the armor has to be as light as possible. Successful solutions often mix several different substances to achieve the best result, Russell notes.

One of the least apparent recent improvements in armor has been the development of new, ultrahigh-hardness (UHH) steels. Such alloys are as much as 20 percent harder than the hardest off-the-shelf high-carbon steels, but they tend to be brittle and can crack when hit. Russell says that Armor Holdings has introduced an optimized version called UH56 steel, which is "hard enough to fracture armor-piercing ammo but tough enough not to crack with many impacts." UH56 is also easier to shape than many of its UHH cousins. The enhanced steels are being installed on many U.S. light-armored vehicles.

Researchers are also working on better transparent materials for windows, which are typically made from multiple laminations of bonded glass. As new threats loom, "the reaction is to add another layer of glass," explains Ron Hoffman of the University of Dayton

Research Institute. But extra glass can make vehicles top-heavy, fuel-thirsty and sluggish.

One promising solution is to replace the glass with significantly cheaper and more effective aluminum oxynitride (ALON), a hard, sapphirelike material developed by industry, the U.S. Army and the U.S. Air Force. ALON offers better protection against armor-piercing projectiles at roughly half the weight and half the thickness of traditional glass-based transparent armor, Hoffman reports.

ALON has been around for years, but it has always been too expensive and too limited in size for vehicle windows. Engineers at Surmet, a ceramics maker in Burlington, Mass., have improved manufacturing processes involving the heating and compressing of ALON powders to make larger pieces of the material and to lower production costs significantly. Still, at around $10 to $15 per square inch, the optical ceramic costs more than military-grade glass ($3 per square inch). Armor Holdings is expected to start installing the lightweight windows this year.

Body armor will soon be in for some significant enhancements as well. Standard–issue ballistic vests, which are reinforced by hard ceramic plate inserts, are massive and bulky but more protective than today's lighter-weight, multilayer fabric alternatives made of woven Kevlar and other high-strength fibers. A new technology called liquid armor may change that, however.

Liquid armor refers to "ballistic fabric infused with a shear-thickening fluid," a substance that stiffens temporarily less than a millisecond after impact, says Norman Wagner, a chemical engineer at the University of Delaware. Co-developed by Wagner's research group and a team led by Eric Wetzel at the U.S. Army Research Lab in Aberdeen, Md., shear-thickening fluid is a mixture of hard nano-particles (often silica or sand) suspended in a nonevaporating liquid such as polyethylene glycol. Although the fluid adds only about 20 percent to the weight of the fabric, it greatly augments its resistance to puncture by high-speed projectiles. It also reduces the effect of blunt trauma by helping to transmit the impact energy to a larger portion of the ballistic fabric, Wagner explains. Certainly, in today's Iraq, allied forces need all the protection they can get.

About the Author

Steven Ashley is a freelance science-technology writer and editor.

New Drone Spies Combat Targets from the Stratosphere

By Larry Greenemeier

Aerial drones have garnered a lot of attention (and controversy) for their ability to launch missile strikes for the U.S. military against enemies in Afghanistan, Pakistan and other hotspots. However, the Department of Defense is now cultivating another type of unmanned aerial vehicle (UAV) for use in combat planning, designed to soar high above the battlefield for so-called ISR (intelligence gathering, surveillance and reconnaissance) missions.

The STS-111 aircraft, which is still in prototype, is in essence a worm-like weather balloon that undulates through the Earth's lower atmosphere, guided by satellite or ground communications or programmed to operate autonomously. "It's really a communications platform that has the ability to provide ISR," says Dan Erdberg, vice president of operations for Sanswire Corp. in Aventura, Fla. Sanswire and Stuttgart, Germany-based TAO Technologies formed a new entity called Sanswire-TAO in June 2008 specifically to develop, market and sell a lineup of ISR UAVs (the STS-111 being their first).

The 33.8-meter long STS-111 is made up of four segments that form what Erdberg refers to as an "airchain" platform. The first segment consists of a bullet-shaped balloon filled with helium, making it lighter than air. The remaining three segments (connected by hinges) house a single, elongated balloon filled with a gaseous fuel made of mostly methane, making it neutrally buoyant (the balloon's mass equals the mass of the air it displaces).

All four segments are contained within a large vented bag that helps the segments move by allowing air to flow in and out. As the aircraft takes off, the gas in each of the balloons expands, forcing air out of the outer bag. At the same time a blower attached under the first segment sends air back into the outer bag. This constant flow of air into and out of the bag creates the motion that helps the

STS-111 gain altitude. A small propeller affixed to the underside of the first segment provides thrust and steering.

When fully inflated the STS-111's widest point is 3.4 meters, and it can carry a payload (cameras and sensors, for example) of up to 9.1 kilograms over a distance of 2,800 kilometers. The aircraft is designed to carry out its missions at altitudes between 3,048 to 9,144 meters.

The Sanswire-TAO aircraft is different from other military drones in several ways, but the two most important are cost and flight duration. Whereas the STS-111 costs about $3 million to make, the Air Force's new "Gorgon Stare" UAV, essentially a Reaper drone fitted with wide-area surveillance sensors, costs about $15 million. And, while a fully loaded Reaper can stay in the air for a maximum of 14 hours, the STS-111 is designed to monitor enemy targets for up to two-and-a-half days before returning to base.

The STS-111 takes off a bit like a kite and can even be launched by a person running in front of it holding an attached rope. Thanks to the helium in the first segment, the aircraft rises, aided by the motion of the remaining three segments. These segments contain no rigid parts; in fact the entire body can be rolled up and stored in a pickup truck bed, according to the company.

Sanswire-TAO announced on Tuesday that they will publicly unveil the STS-111 UAV at Sanford International Airport in Orlando, Fla., in mid-2010. The company, which held a private demonstration of the technology in Stuttgart, Germany, on December 18, is working on a number of what it refers to as "Stratellite" aircraft, with STS-111 being the first. The next Stratellite is expected to fly as high as 18,288 meters.

About the Author

Larry Greenemeier is the associate editor of technology for Scientific American, *covering a variety of tech-related topics, including biotech, computers, military tech, nanotech and robots.*

Will Neuroweapons, Micro-Drones and Other Killer Apps Really Make Us Safer?

By John Horgan

A year ago historians of technology Lee Vinsel and Andrew Russell, my colleagues at Stevens Institute of Technology, questioned our culture's adulation of "innovation" in an essay in Aeon. They titled the essay "Hail the Maintainers," because the flip side of innovation veneration is neglect of maintenance needed to keep societies running. Science and technology scholars explored this theme further at "The Maintainers," a conference held at Stevens (which I reported on here). Although Andy left Stevens last summer and Lee is leaving soon, they organized a follow-up conference, "The Maintainers II," held at Stevens this week (April 6-9). Below is a 10-minute talk I'm giving on military innovation.

–John Horgan

The late psychedelic philosopher Terence McKenna was one of my favorite thinkers. Epic doses of DMT and psilocybin helped him figure out the meaning of existence: The world was designed to produce innovation for our delectation.

Maybe innovation is a divine creative principle. Who knows? But Andy Russell and Lee Vinsel are right: innovation-worship has gotten out of hand. Our obsession with novelty fuels the replication crisis in science and the high costs of health care, among other problems.

Today, I'll focus on an especially insidious kind of innovation, involving war. I used to live across the Hudson River from the U.S. Military Academy at West Point. It has a museum that documents, proudly, our increasingly ingenious methods of killing each other. They range from spears and crossbows up through machine guns, tanks and Fat Man, the bomb that devastated Nagasaki.

Seeking Killer Apps

The U.S. is by far the world's dominant arms producer, peddler and innovator, and it's always trying to extend its lead. The Pentagon has been reaching out to high-tech companies in Silicon Valley and elsewhere for help in creating "disruptive" weaponry. The so-called Defense Innovation Unit-Experimental, DIU-X, has opened offices in Palo Alto, Boston and Austin to solicit proposals from companies and universities. Here's how it describes its mission:

"DIU-X continuously iterates on how best to identify and contract novel innovation... with the ultimate goal of accelerating this technology into the hands of the men and women in uniform." The Defense Department isn't content with slaughtering the English language. Here are a few killer apps I find especially worrisome.

Micro-Drone Assassins

First, drones. The U.S. has deployed a variety of drones for spying and killing. They range from the Global Hawk, with a 130-foot wingspan, to the Switchblade, a baguette-size drone that packs a grenade-size explosive. Research is under way on micro-drones that mimic birds and bugs and can be released in swarms.

The U.S. has catalyzed an international arms race. According to security analyst Peter Singer of the New America Foundation, scores of countries and groups have deployed drones, and many–notably China, Russia and Israel–have their own drone industries.

A few years ago, on assignment for *National Geographic*, I flew a military-grade drone with an eight-foot wingspan. I almost crashed it, but soon any idiot will be able to fly a drone. Just click a location on your hand-held map display, and the drone will fly there and spy on it or blow it up. Drones are being equipped with software that can recognize faces and license plates.

Brain Science and Bionic Soldiers

Second example: brain science. In his book *Mind Wars*, bioethicist Jonathan Moreno of the University of Pennsylvania documents the military's long-standing interest in "neuroweapons." Decades ago, the U.S. explored the potential of psychedelics like LSD and BZ for interrogating, brainwashing and disabling enemies.

The Pentagon is more eager than ever to exploit brain science, according to Moreno. In 2011, the DOD spent more than $350 million on cognitive neuroscience, and that doesn't count black-budget spending.

The Defense Department has provided roughly half the funding for Obama's federal Brain Initiative. The initiative supports research on the brain's software, or neural code, and on technologies like optogenetics, an implantable method for manipulating neurons.

If scientists crack the neural code, all sorts of sci-fi scenarios become possible, including technologies for mind-reading, mind-control and mind-enhancement. As a U.S. Army publication put it recently: "Advances in brain science could lead to improvements in performance and decision making, changing the way soldiers fight in the near future."

Far from questioning the wisdom of such research, leading neuroscientists encouraged colleagues to jump on the defense gravy train in the 2009 report *Opportunities in Neuroscience for Future Army Applications*. Authors include Floyd Bloom and Michael Gazzaniga, former members of the U.S. Council on Bioethics.

Weaponizing brain science could lead to bionic super-soldiers, among other disruptive innovations. How ethical is that?

A New Nuclear Arms Race

My last example involves nuclear weapons. Obama, who won a Nobel Peace Prize for envisioning the abolition of nuclear weapons, signed off on a program to upgrade our nuclear arsenal at a cost of $1 trillion over several decades. Obama sold the program as maintenance of aging facilities and weapons, but it involves plenty of innovation.

Submarine-launched nuclear warheads are being tipped with fuzes that make them more lethal to hardened targets, such as missile silos and underground command-and-control centers. According to *The Bulletin of Atomic Scientists*, the fuzes would allow the U.S. to carry out a pre-emptive strike against Russia with less fear of retaliation.

Our upgrade will "require Russia to undertake countermeasures that would further increase the already dangerously high readiness of Russian nuclear forces." So the U.S. modernization of its nuclear arsenal could provoke a dangerous new arms race and undermine anti-proliferation efforts. Is that good innovation?

Can Weapons Innovation Be Stopped?

Considering the stakes involved, weapons innovation has provoked little serious criticism. Yes, thousands of scientists and engineers, including Stephen Hawking and Elon Musk, have signed a letter calling for a ban on autonomous weapons. But we should be debating military innovation in general, not just killer robots.

When scholars address the issue, their criticism is often muted. In 2015 Stevens hosted a lecture by Yale management professor Paul Bracken. His talk was an awkward mixture of concern and cheerleading. He warned that arms innovation is "racing ahead of strategy," and that novel weapons might make the world more dangerous.

But he also emphasized that the Pentagon, "the mother of all VC firms," is providing terrific opportunities for researchers and investors. Scholars like Bracken probably worry that if they sound too dovish, they'll hurt their chances of getting grants, consulting gigs and conference invitations.

Other scholars extol the benefits of war research, and even war itself. Economist Tyler Cowen of George Mason argues that war, or the threat thereof, improves nations' "long-term prospects" by boosting innovation and economic growth. I find this thesis morally repulsive. It's akin to arguing for the economic benefits of slavery.

Forget morality. From a strictly practical point of view, military innovation, even if it provides short-term advantages for the U.S., ultimately makes the world more dangerous. No society has ever maintained a monopoly on novel weapons.

I wish technology scholars would give arms innovation the scrutiny it deserves. Perhaps they can propose ways in which weapons research can be wound down, as part of a larger goal of winding down war. This issue is too urgent for scholarly neutrality.

All progress begins with wishful thinking. I wish for a future in which weapons of war exist only in museums. Wouldn't that be a trip?

The views expressed are those of the author(s) and are not necessarily those of Scientific American.

About the Author

John Horgan directs the Center for Science Writings at the Stevens Institute of Technology. His books include The End of Science, The End of War *and* Mind-Body Problems, *available for free at mindbodyproblems.com. For many years he wrote the popular blog* Cross Check *for* Scientific American.

GLOSSARY

autonomous Existing or acting separately from other things or people.

causeway A raised road or path that goes across wet ground or water.

combatant A person, group, or country that fights in a battle or war.

cybersecurity The practice of protecting sensitive information from digital attacks.

cyborg A person whose body contains mechanical or electrical devices.

electrodes The points through which electricity flows into or out of a battery or other device.

firmware Computer programs that are contained permanently in a device.

fodder Material that is used for a particular purpose.

geostationary Relating to a satellite that always remains in the same spot over Earth.

hypersonic Relating to speed that is at least five times that of the speed of sound.

kinetic Of or relating to the movement of physical objects.

lethality The capacity to cause great harm, destruction, or death.

manifold Many and various.

neurons Cells that carry messages between the brain and other parts of the body.

payload The things, such as passengers or bombs, that are carried by an aircraft or spacecraft.

propaganda False or exaggerated statements that are spread in order to help a cause, a political leader, or a government.

reconnaissance Military activity in which information about an enemy is gathered.

redux Brought back.

robust Successful or impressive and not likely to fail or weaken.

sanctions Actions that are taken in order to force a country to obey international laws.

FURTHER INFORMATION

Atherton, Kelsey D. "How a robotic arm could help the US Army lift artillery shells," *Popular Science*, December 12, 2022, https://www.popsci.com/technology/us-army-robot-artillery-loader/.

Bowden, Mark. "The Tiny and Nightmarishly Efficient Future of Drone Warfare," *The Atlantic*, November 2022, https://www.theatlantic.com/technology/archive/2022/11/russia-ukraine-war-drones-future-of-warfare/672241/.

Greenemeier, Larry. "When Hatred Goes Viral: Inside Social Media's Efforts to Combat Terrorism," *Scientific American*, May 24, 2017, https://www.scientificamerican.com/article/when-hatred-goes-viral-inside-social-medias-efforts-to-combat-terrorism/.

Poole, Thom. "The myth and reality of the super soldier," BBC News, February 8, 2021, https://www.bbc.com/news/world-55905354.

Rhen, Brad. "Pennsylvania Guard Soldiers Train with new Robotic System," U.S. Army, November 9, 2022, https://www.army.mil/article/261970/pennsylvania_guard_soldiers_train_with_new_robotic_system.

Shepherd, Tory. "'Life no longer as we know it': war in space would have devastating effects, military experts say," *The Guardian*, November 28, 2022, https://www.theguardian.com/science/2022/nov/29/life-no-longer-as-we-know-it-war-in-space-would-have-immediate-effects-expert-says.

Sherman, Jason. "Russia-Ukraine Conflict Prompted U.S. to Develop Autonomous Drone Swarms, 1,000-Mile Cannon," *Scientific American*, February 14, 2022, https://www.scientificamerican.com/article/russia-ukraine-conflict-prompted-u-s-to-develop-autonomous-drone-swarms-1-000-mile-cannon/.

CITATIONS

1.1 New "Symbiote" May Protect Microchips from Cyber Attack by Charles Q. Choi (December 1, 2012); 1.2 The Fog of Cyberwar: What Are the Rules of Engagement? by Larry Greenemeier (June 13, 2011); 1.3 Hacking the Lights Out by David M. Nicol (July 1, 2011); 1.4 Russia's Information War Is Being Waged on Social Media Platforms by Sophie Bushwick (March 8, 2022); 1.5 Russian Misinformation Seeks to Confound, Not Convince by David Robert Grimes (March 28, 2022); 2.1 War of the Machines by P. W. Singer (July 1, 2010); 2.2 The Drone Wars: 9/11-Inspired Combat Leans Heavily on Robot Aircraft by Larry Greenemeier (September 2, 2011); 2.3 Terminate the Terminators by the Editors (July 1, 2010); 2.4 Are Cyborg Warriors a Good Idea? by John Horgan (February 9, 2019); 2.5 Don't Let Robots Pull the Trigger by the Editors (March 1, 2019); 2.6 Are Military Bots the Best Way to Clear Improvised Explosive Devices? by Larry Greenemeier (November 3, 2010); 2.7 To Clear Deadly Land Mines, Science Turns to Drones and Machine Learning by Andrew Robinson and Dominic Smith (September 7, 2022); 2.8 AI-Influenced Weapons Need Better Regulation by Branka Marijan (March 30, 2022); 3.1 Shocking Pink: An Inexpensive Test for Chemical Weapon Attacks y by Larry Greenemeier (March 15, 2012); 3.2 How Can Minute Quantities of Chemicals Such as Sarin Overwhelm the Nervous System of an Adult Human So Quickly? by Michael Allswede (June 7, 2004); 3.3 Fake Botox, Real Threat by Ken Coleman and Raymond A. Zilinskas (June 1, 2010); 3.4 AI Drug Discovery Systems Might Be Repurposed to Make Chemical Weapons, Researchers Warn by Rebecca Sohn (April 21, 2022); 3.5 Is Bird Flu Waiting to Explode? by Fred Guterl (June 1, 2012); 4.1 The Physics and Hype of Hypersonic Weapons by David Wright and Cameron Tracy (August 1, 2021); 4.2 Hypersonic Weapons Can't Hide from New Eyes in Space by Jason Sherman (January 18, 2022); 4.3 How Do We Prevent War in Space? by Ann Finkbeiner (November 1, 2020); 4.4 Space Wars - Coming to the Sky Near You? by Theresa Hitchens (March 1, 2008); 4.5 Enhanced Armor by Steven Ashley (May 15, 2006); 4.6 New Drone Spies Combat Targets from the Stratosphere by Larry Greenemeier (December 31, 2009): 4.7 Will Neuroweapons, Micro-Drones and Other Killer Apps Really Make Us Safer? by John Horgan (April 7, 2017)

Each author biography was accurate at the time the article was originally published.

INDEX